Twelve Dates of Christmas

Twelve Dates of Christmas

A Northampton Hearts Romance

Charlee James

TULE
PUBLISHING

Dedication

For Kendall and Annika
Live how you want, love who you want, and know down to the
tips of your toes you are and always will be cherished beyond
measure.—Mom

Dear Readers,

I hope you enjoy this sweet holiday romance as much as I enjoyed writing it. Winter is one of my favorite times of the year. I love the lights, the excitement, and the snow (although my husband says this is only because he's shoveling it—he's probably right!). I'm forever thankful for my readers, and for the authors who create stories for us bookworms to devour on cozy, snowy days.

Reading has always been my first passion. I find getting lost in someone else's world to be the perfect escape, and it's an honor and a wish come true to share my books with you.

Wishing you and yours all of the love and warmth of the holidays year-round.

xoxo,
Charlee

Chapter One

"Nothing warmed her heart quite like chilly temperatures, icicles, and snowflakes. Significant other? Optional. Perfect mitten and scarf set? Essential."
—The Twelve Dates of Christmas *by Paige Turner*

CHRISTMASTIME WAS ALIVE in the artsy town of North-ampton, Massachusetts. If the glittering lights winding up the trees or the scent of peppermint mocha from the local coffeehouse wasn't enough of an indicator, the weather certainly was. It was freaking cold, but it was hard to care about rosy cheeks and chilly toes when the downtown shops were glowing with holiday cheer.

Grace McGovern's teeth chattered as she crossed the redbrick street with nearly as many shopping bags as her best friend and roommate, Beth Harris.

"Remind me again why we don't do our holiday shopping in August?" Beth grumbled, knotting her scarf more tightly around her neck.

"Because then we'd miss out on all of this." The bags swayed on her arms as she gestured widely at the snow globe around them. Brick-and-mortar shops, each more unique than the next, lined the streets offering one-of-a-kind treasures from local artisans. Cheerful window displays made

Grace's heart swoon with the magic of Christmastime.

"Frostbite?" Beth raised a brow, but smiled all the same.

"Oh, come on. You love it just as much as I do." She gave her friend a playful hip bump as they continued to walk through the snowy streets. Grace stopped to peer into the florist's window display where a thick bed of holly mingled with pine-accented roses. Golden ornaments made it all come together with a dash of elegance.

"*No one* loves the holidays as much as you do." Beth looped her arm through Grace's and gave a gentle tug. "Come on, let's stop into the jewelry store before it closes."

Wind tangled in her hair as thick flakes floated down from the sky like feathers from a burst pillow. She breathed in the fresh air, loving the crisp and clean snap to it. "I know, I know. I was the one who was late coming from work."

"How *is* work?" Beth asked, gripping the shop's door handle. The bells hanging on the door clinked together as they stepped inside and stomped their boots on the welcome mat. A glorious rush of heat enveloped them in the toasty-warm store. All of the glass displays were hand painted in lace patterns that looked like frost forming at the corners of the cases. Silver ornaments and tiny lights dripped from the ceiling like icicles.

"Hmm. It's been an eventful week—kidney stone blogs for a urologist and a few press releases to bury some unflattering news about a selectman in our neighboring town."

"Who knew marketing could be so glamorous?" Beth laughed, then her blue eyes widened, and she rubbed her hands together. A sure sign that Hawk-eyes had spotted the perfect gift for someone.

Grace followed her across the room, luminous treasures catching the overhead lights, casting rainbows in every direction.

Beth admired a long pendant necklace. "Maybe if you took on fewer clients, you'd have time to write a second book." *This again.*

"You know I can't resist the lure of writing snappy secondhand car ads. Besides, I don't have another book in me. That was just for fun." She shrugged under her friend's intense gaze.

"Fun that became a mass-market best seller." Beth rolled her eyes to the ceiling.

"Thanks to all those forlorn daters out there." She busied herself looking at a pair of dangling reindeer earrings. They were so outrageous, they made her laugh.

"Seriously. Why can't I meet a guy who will sweep me off my feet with *The Twelve Dates of Christmas*?" Beth's pink lips puffed into an indignant pout.

"Because it's entirely fictional. And besides, you have Jim, who is quite lovely by the way." She loved working in marketing, but a few years ago she'd gotten the itch to write a Christmastime romance novel. One where the heroine is enthralled by the hero's downright inspiring, thoughtful, and well, totally not real-life date ideas. Readers ate it up like a bag of Lindor chocolate truffles. The experience was fun, but she'd decided after the fourth round of revisions with her editor, she preferred reading books over writing them.

"Which reminds me, I have to get back to the apartment," Beth said, checking her watch. "Jim's stopping by when I get out of work." She fiddled with a pulled string on her scarf, and Grace's lip twitched. Who would've guessed that Beth—the woman who had nerves of steel and bulldozed through anything that stood in her way—would be riddled with nerves over a man? She was happy her friend had finally met her match.

"I still need to pick up a few last-minute Christmas gifts." Grace followed her up to the cashier to chat while Beth paid for her purchase. "Should I make myself scarce when I return?" She smiled, unable to resist teasing Beth just a bit. Jim was Beth's brother's BFF and the person she was never supposed to fall for. Whoops.

"Oh, shush." Beth elbowed her as she removed her wallet, making Grace laugh.

"Sorry. I can't help it." After they thanked the shop owner, they exited through the glass door. The whoosh of frigid air was pins and needles against her face.

"Sure you want to brave the cold? Feels like its dropped below zero." Beth rubbed her hands up and down her arms, face contorted in discomfort.

Grace tapped on her phone to look at the time. Shoot. Only a half hour before the store she needed to get to closed. "Yeah. I love this stuff. See you back at the apartment in an hour or so." They went their separate ways, Beth to their apartment on the next block while Grace rushed to the toy store. Her boots fluffed up the powdery snow as she dashed to Toy Town, a super cute kids' store on the corner of Main Street. Her younger sister, Nora—much younger—still lived at home as a first grader should. Nora loved the heck out of these plastic beasts that extricated sparkly slime, and she was ready to rise to the occasion of best sister by getting her the latest blind box. The big *surprise* was how your slime would be revealed—an explosion of sewer sauce or a flying snot rocket. Gag.

The doorbell chimed and sugar-scented heat enveloped her. The source of the delicious smell was frosted cookies set out for shoppers. There were only a couple left on the plate. She shouldn't, but she hadn't eaten dinner after all. She snagged a treat in one hand—she *had* walked across the street—and looped a shopping basket around her forearm.

"Hey, we're closing in twenty-five."

She spared a glance toward the sullen voice to see a circa 2012 Justin Bieber lookalike. His arms were crossed over his varsity football sweatshirt, hip cocked against the checkout desk.

"Great. Thanks." She took a bite of the cookie and picked up her pace so someone—no names—wouldn't get their jockstrap in a bunch. She started at the far corner and went up the aisle.

A man standing in the middle of the carpeted row let out a labored sigh and pushed his glasses up the bridge of his nose, only to have them slide back down. Cute. Totally out of his element. His dark hair fluffed out at odd angles, like he'd raked his hands through it too many times. And his clothes…well, matching wasn't included in his packet of man skills. Right now there was a coordinating conundrum of epic proportion—gray dress pants and a khaki-colored shirt. His bottom half said board meeting, while the top half said safari exploration. Perhaps he was a bit colorblind. He was tall, with at least a foot on her, which wasn't too hard when you barely reached five foot one in heels. He picked up a baby doll, examined it like it was a tissue sample from another planet, and returned it to the shelf. Poor guy. She brushed off her jacket to make sure no crumbs had settled there and cleared her throat to alert him of her presence.

"Guess you're not looking for Really Wets Winnie, huh?" she asked, glancing at the doll's packaging.

"Huh? Oh, no. I'm not." Another sigh escaped from his lips, and she couldn't stop the little pang of pity from sparking in her chest.

"Well, what are you looking for?" she asked, smiling as he fished through his coat pocket and pulled out a scrap of paper.

"Pixie Princesses—more specifically 'Enchanted Water' and 'Blooming Blossom' editions. Guess I'm out of luck." His shoulders sagged slightly. His body language was so comical she nearly laughed. Still, he was pretty darn handsome in a cute-nerd sort of way and looked like he'd rather be anywhere else in the world than the toy shop.

"No, you're just in the wrong aisle." She stepped closer, catching the fresh, clean notes of his aftershave.

"Oh, you work here? Thanks. I couldn't find anyone earlier." The relief in his voice was audible, and he relaxed a fraction.

Was this guy for real? She was wearing a winter coat and boots. "You mean Captain Sunshine didn't offer to lend a hand?"

"Who?"

"Ah, nothing." He didn't catch her sarcasm. She reached into her jacket pocket to peek at her cell phone. Eighteen minutes. "Just a last-minute holiday shopper like you. Come on, we're headed to the same destination." She gestured down the aisle with her hand, and he fell into line beside her. Who knew what would happen to him if she didn't take him under her wing?

"I figured I could get them through Amazon Prime, but when I went to order this morning, they were out of stock. I can't disappoint my two nieces."

"Don't look so defeated yet. My sister likes that set too. Almost as much as her slime beasts, but they are popular," she said, waving her hands as she spoke, even with the cookie and basket still in her grasp. They walked along the shop's back wall until they reached the aisle with the collectibles.

"How old is your sister?" he asked, scanning the shelves with the most vibrant green eyes she'd ever seen.

"Seven. Her birth was immaculate conception though." She was happy to have a sibling, but she didn't want to think of all the gory details that might've transpired right down the hall from her bedroom.

The man beside her laughed. The sound reverberated off the walls and warmed through her like hot chocolate. His wide shoulders shook beneath his winter coat. She liked to make people smile, even at her own expense. She especially liked the way the stranger's Adam's apple bobbed along his throat, and the dimples that popped in his cheeks when he grinned like that. Super cute.

Too bad she was on a dating hiatus. It was for the best though. Her last date six months ago had taken her to a cheap steakhouse and asked if she could finish the Cowboy's Blue-Ribbon flank steak—*free* if you consumed the whole sixteen-ounce slab. He wouldn't have to pay, and she could get her picture on the wall. *Not happening.* She had declined the case of the meat sweats and a second date. The event described her romantic life to a T. Nonexistent. She just wanted to find what her parents had. After all these years, they were still deeply in love, and her dad was super romantic—always surprising her mom with the sweetest gestures and dates to let her know he cared.

"You're funny." He stretched out his hand. "I'm Owen Ellis. Thanks for helping me out. Sadie and Selina will appreciate it."

"Grace McGovern." She clasped his hand in a quick shaking motion. "Don't thank me yet though. The shelves look a bit sparse, and we're on a time crunch." She started taking down boxes of dolls and other packaged items on the display. Usually people didn't put things back in the right space. She'd leave it nicer than she found it, despite Bieber's foul disposition.

Grace let out a victory whoop when her hand closed around a pink box. "Blooming Blossom." She handed the package behind her without looking and frowned. There weren't any other boxes like it, and he still needed one more. "Looks like it's the last one." She stood on her tiptoes to reach the gift for her sister, and suddenly he was right behind her, lending a long arm to remove the slime beasts from the top shelf.

"Thanks all the same. One down, one to go." His eyebrows rose as he looked at the slime beasts package. "Those do what?" He crinkled his nose, and she chuckled.

"The big reveal is whether they poop or snot out the slime. If you get super lucky, your beast will toss its cookies.

That means you've got an ultra-rare on your hands." She pointed to that little detail on the package.

"How is that lucky?" He shook his head incredulously, looking totally befuddled by the gift.

"They're all the rage among the elementary school population." She skirted to the side to allow a woman escorting a trio of excited children to pass: a parade of puffed coats, red cheeks, and pom-pom topped woolen hats. "I guess body humor will never not be funny."

"Looks messy," he said, lifting his chin toward the package. His eyes twinkled with humor as he rocked back on his heels.

"Ah, well." She sighed. "We throw plastic covers over anything we hold dear."

His lips twitched. "What happened to the run-of-the-mill jack-in-the-box?" He shook his head, feigning dismay.

She shrugged. "At least the world has Pixie Princesses. Come on, let's see if someone put more in another aisle by mistake." When they didn't find any others, she went to the counter, unable to give up on the mission to help this nice uncle find the toy his other niece wanted.

"Hi. We were hoping you might have an Enchanted Water Pixie." The look the Bieber wannabe cast her was that of total disdain.

He shrugged, glancing at his watch. "Yeah, probably."

"Okay," she said when he didn't make any attempt to move. "So can you get it for us?"

"Listen, we close in ten minutes, and it's out back, so you'll have to return another time." He tossed his hair, even though it was cemented in place by gel.

"Unless the 'out back' you're referring to is the land Down Under, I don't think it will take ten minutes to walk to the back room." She echoed his stance, arms crossed, hip cocked. The kid rolled his eyes and turned to the door directly behind him. Not exactly a ten-minute walk.

"You know you're kind of a bully, right?" Owen whispered, leaning slightly toward her. Whatever scent he was wearing made her want to bury her face in the material of his shirt. A hint of balsam. Maybe citrus.

"You'll thank me in five minutes." His smile grew wider, the thump of her heart faster. She was used to getting what she wanted. Convincing businesses of the marketing packages that would lead them to their goals wasn't for the faint of heart, but she was up to the challenge, and to this day not one of her clients had regretted spending a little extra to get results for their product or business.

She wasn't sure when dimples had become so dazzling, but it was her new favorite feature of the opposite sex. Or maybe he just wore them well.

WHEN THE KID reappeared one minute and thirty seconds later with the Enchanted Water Pixie, she couldn't help but gloat a bit as Owen stared down at her with a satisfied grin. Camaraderie buzzed between them, and maybe a little something more. They paid for their respective purchases and walked out the door. The second they stepped foot on the concrete, the dead bolt was engaged and the Open sign was flipped to Closed. She and Owen dissolved into a fit of laughter.

"I'd hate to be that kid's high school teacher," he said, still chuckling. "Thanks for your help today. I think it's safe to say I wouldn't have found these without you."

"Not a chance." Her brain suddenly registered that her cheeks ached from smiling. They hadn't gotten this type of workout in a long time. "We got them just in the nick of time too." They grinned at each other, for one lingering beat, then two, three. Until Owen cleared his throat. The sound brought her attention to his mouth. His top lip was slightly narrower than the bottom, supple, with a pinkish hue. She forced her eyes up over his perfectly symmetrical face: clear, smoothly shaven skin, a straight nose, and imposing brows that offset his clear eyes. And she had a thing for the sexy nerd glasses. Starting now.

Snowflakes swirled around them, landing on his broad shoulders. "I, ah… You wouldn't want to grab a hot chocolate," he stated more than asked, shifting around a bit. "Would you?"

She bit her lower lip to keep from chuckling, afraid he'd think she was teasing him instead of understanding what was really on her mind. The fact that he seemed to have no game when it came to women was refreshing. Slick pick-up lines were not her thing.

"Yes, I think I would." She tossed some of her scraggly curls behind her, suddenly feeling self-conscious. She wasn't wearing any makeup, and beneath her coat she was sporting a *cats-coffee-books* sweatshirt. If that didn't spell middle-aged spinster in the making, she didn't know what did.

"Awesome." He beamed down at her, looking like she'd

made his whole week by agreeing to consume a hot beverage with him. Warmth slowly spread through her chest. Being able to have that effect on someone was a really nice feeling. Unexpected. She wanted to get to know him, almost as much as she wanted that hot chocolate.

If she could count on history to repeat itself, though, this would just be another ho-hum holiday fling.

Chapter Two

"Her personality was sweet and warm, so on the first date of Christmas, hot cocoa shared fireside was the natural choice. (Hint: accompanying bakery treat is a must.)"

—The Twelve Dates of Christmas *by Paige Turner*

O WEN SNUCK A glimpse at the woman walking next to him. He wasn't exactly sure where he'd gotten the guts to ask her out. Maybe it was because his feet had frozen to the toy shop floor, momentarily stunned by her pretty mocha eyes, her bouncy curls, and most of all, her smile. One that was good-natured and helpful. One that melted away his reserves about talking with a beautiful stranger. He was far more comfortable with computers and coding than he was with women. He was completely clueless when it came to the opposite sex. At least his last girlfriend had thought so—her parting gift to him had been a romance novel chucked in his general direction. She'd marched out the door muttering that he needed all the help he could get. He still didn't understand where he'd gone wrong.

For the past year he'd thrown himself into work, proving his ex's point. He did thrive on the routine of going into the office, and once he was there, he often stayed well past five o'clock. He didn't consider himself a workaholic, but when he got wrapped up in a project, it fascinated him. This was the first time since the fateful book assault that he'd gone on a date—if hot chocolate was considered a date. Was it? See? Clueless. He sucked at reading social cues.

She shivered beside him, sinking down into the belted jacket that hit right above the knees. The quilted fabric was the color of the cardinals that perched on the silver birch trees outside of his home. Grace was true to her namesake, moving with a quick lightness much like the little fledglings that flitted beyond his window. Beautiful, created to stand out among all the other birds. A striking scarlet that could never fade into the background—that was her. A plain winter wren had no business perching on a branch with a cardinal.

"The town did such an amazing job with the lights this year," she said through chattering teeth as they navigated the icy sidewalks to the coffeehouse.

"Did you grow up here?" He hovered his hand behind her elbow as they crossed an icy patch on the concrete.

"We moved twice growing up, but always in New England. My best friend and I both work in town—I'm in marketing; she's an accountant—and we rent an apartment together. What about you? Native or transplant?"

"I'm originally from Connecticut. Not too far from here, but my job at New England Engineering brought me north." The big brass teakettle that hung above the entrance swayed as he opened the door.

Grace paused, eyes fluttering closed. Her chest rose as she inhaled, and a soft sigh flowed from her lips. The pretty sound of pure pleasure was warmed honey settling in his stomach. He swallowed hard.

"I've never made it in here. It smells amazing." Their boots thudded against the gray-washed wooden floors to a counter constructed of faded brick. Caged Edison bulbs washed the place in a dusky glow, highlighting the mismatched sofas and armchairs in a rainbow of muted colors. Tables for two were tucked into private window alcoves, letting in natural light and the view of powdered snow whirling beyond the glass. Someone had scrawled the menu on the black chalkboard, describing the giant confections and baked goods that tempted from a glass display case. A treasure trove of icing, sprinkles, and cinnamon swirl.

"What are you thinking?" He followed her eyes to the board she was intently reading.

"I'm overwhelmed with hot cocoa flavors." She glanced up at him and grinned, and for a second he was breathless, nearly dizzy with it. So pretty. "What's your favorite?"

"Classic. It's the only one I've actually had." He found himself smiling again, enjoying the way her eyes widened at the display of sweets.

"Oh man. Where can I get a job application? I want to spend the rest of my days lusting over Boston cream pie and pink French macarons." She licked her bottom lip, and it did funny things to his heart rate. The quick clip pounding against his rib cage and the double beat made him take pause. *Thirty-five is too young to have a heart attack.* The mental reassurance was only moderately comforting. When the cashier pulled a cinnamon bun the size of a dinner plate out of the warmer then slathered the thing with cream cheese frosting, the longing on her face made him jealous. Of a pastry. If she ever looked at him like that, he'd need to find a good cardiologist. Immediately.

"I take it you're getting the cinnamon bun." He chuckled, but there was nothing remotely funny about the way Grace's eyes looked when she wanted something.

"I shouldn't." She breathed, shaking her head with regret. An espresso machine hissed behind the counter, and the barista added a swirl of caramel to the top of a beverage.

"You really should." Anything that put that look on her face she should have. Right away.

"My resolve is weak. Will you share it with me?" She looked up at him from lush lashes that were a few shades darker than her eyes.

"Yes. Why don't you get a table, and I'll surprise you on the hot chocolate flavor?" Oh man. He didn't know what she'd like. Why had he said that? Spontaneity wasn't him.

"Deal. I'll be over there in one of those neat little nooks, which by the way will be my designated break area once I secure employment." She started to turn, then stopped and fished through her shoulder bag. "Here's my half."

"No way." He took a step back from the money she held out, shaking his head. "I asked you here." At least that much he could figure out.

She paused momentarily, mouth open as if she was going to protest. He wasn't letting her go dutch on this might-be-a-date. She stuck the money back into her wallet, and her expression softened. "Thanks," she said and stepped out of line and walked to the table she'd pointed out before.

When it was his turn in line, he ordered the cinnamon

roll, four hot chocolates, and two empty mugs. One of each flavor so she could try them all and decide which one she liked best. Kind of like a wine tasting, but with hot cocoa. Was that dumb? He didn't think of fun ideas on the fly. He was trying to impress her, because he liked her. He'd either crash and burn or set unrealistic expectations. The thought made him more determined. He was intelligent and successful. Maybe she would go on a second date.

It was another minute or so before the order was ready, and he headed to the table with a giant tray. Heaviness settled in his stomach. She was going to think this was ridiculous, and it wasn't like he could ditch the tray and bring over one mug—he was already in her line of sight. She'd removed her coat and was wearing a sweater the color of the pink macarons behind the glass. The material hugged her beautiful curves and looked like it would be soft to the touch. He set down the cinnamon roll, followed by the tall mugs of hot cocoa down the center of the table, and swallowed hard. Once he was free of the tray, he shoved off his own jacket and busied himself hanging it on the hook beside hers. He pulled out the high back burgundy chair and sat against the crushed velvet upholstery. Her seat was also an accent chair, but that's where the similarities ended. The fabric Grace was sitting against was a burst of yellow embroidered with white swans. Of course it had to be swans. It was too fitting.

"Whoa," she said, looking at him with an expression that could only be described as pure delight. The tension in his muscles loosened. *She likes it.* Her eyes squinted as she smiled, alive with an inner glow of light that nearly knocked him off his feet.

"Which is which?" she asked, eyes scanning over the choices on the table. A fluttering erupted in his gut, and he tried to get past the dry, choked feeling in his throat. *Don't. Screw. Up.*

"Okay," he said on a long breath. "This one here with the marshmallow and chocolate bar skewer is the s'mores. This one is peppermint mocha." He pointed to the glass with fresh whipped cream drizzled in hot fudge and garnished with a large chunk of peppermint bark and got great pleasure when her mouth went slack. "Then our last two contenders are gingerbread and classic." A cheery-looking gingerbread man clung to the glass with one arm, the rest of its buttery, baked body was floating on a pillow of whipped cream. The classic was his favorite flavor—he could tell before tasting the others. It had just the right amount of chocolate and little marshmallows floating on top. Classic, boring, vanilla, safe. He'd been described as those things more than once.

"You've done prison time," Grace blurted out, then leaned in, eyes narrowed and suspicious.

"What?" He laughed, then sobered when her face remained expressionless and cleared his throat. "Ah, no."

She pursed her lips and double-tapped her chin. "You're allergic to cats." She tilted her head, curls spilling over her sweater, which did indeed have a feline perched in the corner near her shoulder.

"Never seemed to be an issue. My mom loves cats, and if I had been allergic, I'm sure our neighbor would've awakened to a baby on their doorstep." Grace was grilling him, and he was actually enjoying himself. She was unusual. Most of his friends were intellects like him. Their idea of fun was building robotics from scratch and battling them in the basement. Grace, of course, seemed like an intelligent person, but one who was much more outgoing, impulsive, and take-charge than anyone he'd ever met.

"Hmm." She let out a thoughtful sigh. "Under tip?" When he shook his head, she continued. "Talk on speaker phone in public places?" His lip twitched at that one. Sometimes he took public transit into Boston, and that really grated his nerves. Apparently, hers too. "Chew with your mouth open?"

His shoulders bounced with humor, and he let out a quick chuff. "Grace, I drive at or below the speed limit, pay my taxes, and I'm a generous tipper. I shovel my driveway and sidewalk, use my turn signal, and if you agree to see me on future occasions, I promise I won't be distracted by my cell phone."

"Have you ever seen that meme? The one that says, 'If you wanna impress me with your car, it better be a food truck?' I kinda feel like you just pulled up and gave me the key." For the first time, she looked a bit bashful and averted her eyes to the drinks on their table.

"A key won't do any good if the food is cold when you get to it." He slid the cinnamon roll toward her, amused at the clear excitement on her face. She cut it into four sections, took one from the plate, then slid it closer so he could take some. Grace lifted the pastry to her mouth and took a sizable bite. "Oh my gosh, I'm ruined for any other baked good." Her long sigh made his pulse jackhammer beneath his skin.

He had to stay focused on impressing her. Had to keep

his cool. "Now, which hot chocolate should we try first?" They were both leaning into the table, holding their pastry in their left hand.

"S'mores," she stated immediately. He liked that she didn't skirt around what she wanted. His ex had constantly given him the cold shoulder or made him choose the restaurant only to fall into an annoyed silence when he picked the wrong thing. He carefully poured the drink into the two empty mugs, placing the skewer in hers.

"Here." She slid a marshmallow and a piece of chocolate off the wooden stick into his cup. "How can you properly judge them if you don't get the full experience?"

"You do have a point there." So, she was thoughtful too.

She took a sip, froze, then went in for another. "Oh yum." Melty chocolate clung to her fingertips as she slid the candy off the skewer and popped it in her mouth. He forgot to swallow, the hot chocolate pooling in his mouth. "I don't think anything can top this one," she sighed.

"Definitely not." But he was looking at her when he said it, drink forgotten on the table. He wasn't even sure he was going to see this woman again. The last half hour had been a whirlwind of fun, with a buzzy feeling of excitement that felt a lot like Christmas morning as a kid. Risk taker he was not. He was the guy who spent months researching reviews and advice before purchasing an armchair, and he had the La-Z-Boy to prove it. He was cautious, liked to determine all the calculations before jumping *feet* first into something. And yet with Grace, he hadn't deliberated before asking her to the café. It was like his heart was shouting *go for it*, while his brain was replaying the moment when Sarah hurled that love story at him and slammed the door on their time together. Maybe he'd be less apprehensive if it was the first time someone said he was hopeless when it came to romance, but it wasn't. He wasn't smooth. He wasn't cool. Yes, he was successful. Had designed safe, stable bridges and infrastructure that could hold up to time's ticking clock. Casanova he was not.

"Okay, you pick now. What's it going to be?" There was a dab of chocolate on her cheek that looked cute rather than messy.

"Gingerbread." And so it went back and forth until the drinks were sampled and the cinnamon bun consumed.

"So, what's your final consensus?" Owen asked Grace as they leaned back in their chairs.

"The one with all the white chocolate peppermint bark. Delicious." To her left, silver snow was still falling over the town, covering the sidewalks in billowy sheets that sparkled under streetlights. "What was yours?"

Classic. "S'mores," he blurted out. He wasn't about to admit that his favorite flavor of ice cream was vanilla and he liked plain cheese pizza. Grace probably dated men who were adventurous, attractive, and exciting. One who would like all the different flavors and textures of a s'mores hot chocolate, while he found it too overpowering. Too explosive. "The original was boring, right?" *Why, why did he have to say that?*

As if reading his mind, she answered, "That hot chocolate was not boring. Besides, things are termed classic because they're reliable choices that you can come back to over and over again. Things that never disappoint. I like classic. Classic is good." Was she onto him? That he was pretending to be more than he was?

Owen cringed at her assessment and how closely it summed up his personality. The last thing he wanted to be was the turnstile of stability. But she had said she liked classic…

"Are you a chronic gambler?" he asked. "Or a part-time jewel thief?"

"Why does it matter?" She smiled, a hint of tease in her tone.

"Just my luck. Which one? I might be able to deal." Kidding. Not kidding.

"Neither." Her grin grew wider. She really did seem to be enjoying herself. He typically bored dates into hibernation.

"Oh no, it's worse, isn't it? You're an avid skydiver?" Risks were meant to be taken with the stock market, not your body.

"Illegal activity is preferable to jumping out of a plane?" One perfectly arched eyebrow rose.

"Any day of the week." He grinned back at her across the table.

"I've only gone skydiving once, and while it was exhilarating, it's not on my list of reoccurring activities. I do like kayaking in the summer, trying new foods, and going to exotic places."

His heart shrank at her words. She was fearless and venturesome. He was the type that preferred a leisurely hike, identifying all the plants and wildlife, while she would be the one free climbing up the side of a mountain. He and Grace were two opposing anodes. Electrons needed to flow from an anode to a cathode. Everyone knew that. They just weren't a compatible match… He was having such a good time though.

"I'd like to get to know you better." His heart was picking up speed. Maybe it was the sugar surge. Maybe it was her.

"Even if I happen to enjoy questionable hobbies?" Her smile turned playful and unconstrained.

"I'm still going to ask." A surge of tingles glimmered through his chest, like the snow whirling around the cheerful cherry bows tied to the lampposts. One of the bows broke free from the post, riding the gust along with the flakes of snow. The red bow tossed and shook down the sidewalk, over the street as the wind and snow kept stirring it up, spinning it this way and that. Not too much different from what he was feeling with Grace. One casual date and she'd shaken him up, spun him around in a whirlwind he didn't quit grasp. She was special. Different.

Was he brave enough to hang on for the ride?

Chapter Three

"Interesting and magical things come alive during the holidays. (Credit card debt, however, also may have a life of its own. And that is certainly not magic.)"
—The Twelve Dates of Christmas *by Paige Turner*

GRACE LEANED BACK in the café chair, considering Owen over the rim of the mug she was holding. She had about one sip left in her before her stomach revolted against all the sweet stuff she'd consumed. *Or better yet, put down the cup now.* Owen was going to ask her out again. She could see it in the way he swallowed hard and looked at her with such intensity she thought she might melt into the chair. She'd been on a few dates but hadn't found the spark she was looking for. She liked her life as it was, even if she didn't have a significant other. Her job was awesome and exciting, she got to live with her very best friend, and they'd had some serious adventures together. In fact, she and Beth had vowed to experience the Christmas "dates" from the book she'd written together, but that was when they were both single. Beth had a sweetie now, and Grace was thrilled for her.

The Twelve Dates of Christmas was part fantasy, and part borrowed from her parents' courtship. She'd grown up on stories of their first Christmas together—horse-drawn sleighs, Christmas markets, and gingerbread houses. In her world—at least the real one—dating had never looked like that, but it was out there. Her parents were living proof. She couldn't deny that something kindled inside her when she looked into Owen's eyes, and she'd love to learn more about the kind of person he was.

Owen had been so considerate since the moment she met him. He opened doors for her, hovered his hand near her arm when they passed over icy spots on the street, and thought of a fun way to sample every hot chocolate in the place. She hadn't felt judged when she'd polished off her half of a ginormous cinnamon roll, and the conversation was playful and easy.

"Just for the record, I'm not a cat burglar and I don't steal parking spaces in a crowded mall. I might've gotten a ticket for letting my parking meter run out of change due to a product launch meeting gone horribly wrong. I'm a bit jaded when it comes to the dating scene, but this has been really nice." She gasped in some air, realized she'd been rambling. Owen didn't seem to mind. He wasn't scrolling through his cell phone or looking at the trio of peppy college-aged women who'd come through the door. His focus was intently locked on her. *Nice* was a perfect way to describe her afternoon. Not nice as in fine or okay or safe. Nice as in uplifting, light, and fun in a really unexpected way. "So when you do ask me on a second date, should you still be considering after learning of my parking infraction, my answer will be yes." She chuckled when his face lit up in an instant like the flip of a switch at the town's tree-lighting ceremony.

"I'm going to let the infraction slide." He laughed. "Grace, I would really like to see you again. Do you have plans for Sunday?"

She'd been expecting him to take her phone number, then wait a week or so until he got around to texting her. She didn't want to be disappointed, but perhaps she should expect the unexpected when it came to Owen.

"Just with a basket of laundry and Netflix. Sunday sounds great." Only after they solidified plans to see each other did he ask for her number. She rattled it off, and he sent her a quick text so she had his number.

You're so pretty. See you Sunday.

She grinned at his text, felt the skin on her cheeks tingle with warmth, and replied to his note.

Sure you're not allergic to cats?

His quick bark of laughter echoed in their private little nook, and he shook his head. "No, not allergic to cats." He reached out his hand, holding his baby finger toward her.

"What?" She laughed. *My sides are beginning to ache.* "Are you trying to pinkie swear me?"

"That's exactly what I'm trying to do, but you're kinda leaving me hanging here." He thrust his hand farther.

Grace let out a mock sigh and slid her tiny pinkie against his much larger one. Her fingers decided this was the exact moment to develop an intense sensitivity to touch, and she suppressed a shiver. Not one from the glacial air permeating the glass, but from Owen and his goofy pinkie swear. "Congratulations. You just got my first pinkie swear in about two decades."

He let out an airy whistle. "Must be hanging around with the wrong crowd."

"First graders?" There was a newfound lightness in her limbs. This was exactly what she needed, even if that second date didn't work out. *Please let it work out.* He'd given her a sliver of carefree time and good company.

"Come on. I'll walk you to your car." He stood up, stacking the trays and glasses to bring to the receptacle, then returned to put on his jacket.

"You don't have to." She fumbled with the last button on her coat and tied the fabric belt at her waist into a loose knot. "I live close to here, so I didn't drive."

"I'll walk you then." He tugged the zipper of a rich indigo puffer jacket that hit just below his hips. The coat suited him. It looked dependable and appealing without unnecessary frills. They both picked up their respective shopping bags. She turned to lead the way to the door, waving him off. "You don't have to. Save yourself the steps and—"

"Please humor me. It's dark out. Plus the snow hasn't let up." The concern in his voice made her take pause. *It is dark and icy.*

"Okay." Grasping the door handle, she pushed outside. The air was frigid and still, the only movement was peaceful snow floating to the earth. The sheen from a patch of ice caught her eye and she turned to warn Owen, but it was too late. He was already sliding but didn't quite lose his balance—yet. She gripped his firm bicep, not that she could hold him up if he went down, but at least she could say she tried. He seemed to regain his footing—until his leg collided with hers and they went down in a flailing heap, a tangle of limbs and winter gear. The hard surface smacked her rear, and she let out a yelp. Pain radiated through her hip and up her back. Well, she hadn't actually anticipated going down with him.

"I'm so sorry. Are you okay?" His panic-stricken tone made her sit up—at least try to. One of his legs was sandwiched between her knees, and there wasn't room between her and the snowbank to get her footing. If she sat up, she'd crush his femur. If he tried to stand first, she'd probably accidently get kicked in the face. "Did you hurt anything?" he asked more insistently.

"If I say yes, will I get another hot chocolate on Sunday?" The snow was melting beneath her gloves and seeping through the material.

"Grace," he said on a heavy sigh edged with concern.

It was his pinched expression that made her stop teasing. "Okay, fine. I'm all right. You?"

He shook his head, and she looked him over more closely. Maybe his leg really had broken the full force of her fall. "No. I'm going to walk you home and then finish my life in a permanent state of shame."

Her shoulders sagged. She hadn't even noticed the tension that ballooned inside her when he said he wasn't okay. "Oh, come on. It wasn't that bad."

"It was so bad that neither of us can get up without making this look like a dirty game of Twister." He glanced over their tangled limbs, and she laughed, accidently snorting in the process.

His face lightened and he chuckled at her. Soon they were sitting there laughing like loons. An older man walked past on the street and raised a questioning brow at them, making them both dissolve into another fit of laughter.

"Okay. Okay," she gasped, holding on to her aching sides. "No more." And then she was folded over again, shaking with silent rolls of comical hysteria. Tears were leaking from her eyes, and she swiped them away with her coat sleeves.

When the laughter finally died down, she looked up at Owen, whose eyes were shining with amusement.

"How about we try standing up before the next wave of laughter leaves us permanently stuck." Instead of drawing away from him, she slid in closer.

"Grace, I really don't think this is the place—" he choked out. Had she ever seen a man get flustered so easily? Well, no. But the reaction was sweet. He was sweet. She liked how he used her name often, infusing it with a lilt of warmth or humor.

"Don't worry. Your honor is safe." The corner of her lip twitched. She'd maneuvered enough to untuck her leg. Her butt was centered on the ice between his legs, her feet on either side of his hips. "Okay, so I'm not a gymnast. Actually I'm not even remotely physically fit. Think you can give me a boost if I push up on your shoulders?"

"I can do that." His voice had dropped a few octaves, eyes locked on hers. A spark crackled inside her as she met his gaze. She'd been wrong about his eyes. They weren't only green, but flecked with tiny slivers of gold, rich and jewel-toned. They sat there for one pulse, then two, as snow sparkled between them and the air grew thick. She was a little breathless, as awareness of how close they were warmed through her. It was a wonder the ice and snow hadn't melted around them. She was totally thrown for a loop. Yes, she'd thought he was adorable and kind, but she hadn't been prepared for the physical jolt he gave her.

She wasn't sure how long they'd been sitting like this, locked in place by the tension-laced currents snapping around them. Her brain suddenly registered the chill of pins and needles against her hands and the backs of her thighs. Time to get off the ice. She put her hands on his shoulders. They were broad and hard beneath her hands—a living, breathing contradiction to all of those stereotypes about smarties. He had the glasses, the brain, and clothing choices of someone who might be dubbed a bit nerdy, but his body was the stuff of fantasies. Hers. She struggled into an intimate and uncomfortable standing position and shifted so both feet were planted on the left side of his body.

"Whew, that was my workout for the month," she joked, hoping to lighten the mood that had hinted to something more, something intense between them. He tried to move, slid a bit, and then stood upright. "Maybe you're the one who needs to be walked home." She gave him a little shoulder bump so he'd know she was joking. He chuckled and the awkward tension dissipated.

"Yeah. That was embarrassing." He scrunched up his face in a cringe.

"Happens to the best of us. Well, except me of course." Her sarcastic sense of humor typically was an acquired taste, but Owen didn't seem fazed by it. He merely laughed at her quips.

"Of course," he said as their boots thudded against the

fresh sugar snow. She couldn't see him well in the dark, but she could detect the smile in his voice. The glow of silver lights hugging the trees along the sidewalk lit their way. *Ethereal* was the only way to describe it, like everything was iced in crystal. A winter wonderland all their own—at least for the moment. The sidewalks were free of other pedestrians who were probably home for the evening, getting cozy and warm over supper.

"This is it." She tilted her head to look up at the brick building. The architecture always drew her. Swan's neck pediments gracing the windows at the top of the building, a roofline framed by an intricate cornice design. She stepped up onto the stoop, and the snow falling over her was suddenly stopped by an iron canopy.

"I was dreading going toy shopping today, but now I'm really glad I did." There were snowflakes stuck to his eyelashes, and dotted through his hair. His glasses were fogging up, but she could still see the sharp jade color of his eyes.

"Me too, even if you did take me out on the ice back there." She regretted her words when his face fell. Okay, so he was sensitive. She'd have to be careful of that in the future, because she did playfully joke—a lot. Her sarcastic sense of humor had gotten her in trouble in the past. Dates would get annoyed or take offense. She'd just write them off as incompatible with her personality. What was different about Owen that made her want to try to consider his feelings? Maybe it was because Owen actually was insecure, and not just a man with an inflated ego to bruise.

He groaned. "Don't remind me. My two left feet are a curse." The snow came down around him, illuminated by the golden sheen of a streetlamp.

"Are you telling me not to bring my salsa heels on Sunday?" She leaned into the iron railing, smiling as she looked down at him.

"That's exactly what I'm saying, because if you see me dance, you'll run." His laugh held a little too much self-deprecation, and she instantly wanted to assure him. Who had made this hot, uber-smart guy second-guess himself at every breath? Because she'd beat them up. She would. She might be a teaser, but she was a staunch advocate of underdogs everywhere. Many of her clients were second-choice consumer brands that needed a push against top competitors like Llama Hummus and Sugar-O's.

"I bet you move just fine." She put a little extra oomph in her statement and looked him over. He was insecure, but he really shouldn't be.

His color in his cheeks, already pink from the wind and snow, deepened. "Right. I'm going to go now. Night, Grace."

"Good night, Owen. Thanks for walking me home. Are you sure I can't drive you to your car?" She bit her bottom lip. Maybe she should insist. How well could he see with those glasses clouded up?

"No, it's not too far from here. Go inside and get warm." His words were soft and caring, and the way he looked at her made her hand tremble against the railing.

They lingered there for another moment, then she turned and opened the door to the main foyer, waving over her shoulder. She stomped her boots, shaking free the snow that clung to her whole lower half, and started up the stairs.

At the halfway point, there was a window framed by rainbow-colored stained glass. She looked out to see Owen still standing below. She knocked on the glass, waving when he looked up at her. He smiled and waved back before starting to walk down the street. When was the last time someone had waited to confirm she'd gotten into her building okay? Owen was considerate, and that went a long way with her. In fact, that's the way her father was too. She continued tromping up the stairs, stomach about to burst because of her evening of gastro indiscretions, and wondered why two women who considered sloths to be their inner avatar would rent an apartment on the third floor in a building with no elevator. It made no sense. She shoved her key in the lock and opened the apartment door.

"Why didn't we rent on a first floor?" she groaned, stepping inside. Apple spice candles and lemon Pledge peppered the air. Telltale smells of one of Beth's frantic cleaning binges, although those were usually reserved for her mother's visits.

"Because Beth's mom said renting on the first floor wasn't safe, and would lead to your untimely demises." Jim didn't even look up from the magazine he was looking at on the couch, but he did smirk. Mrs. Randall was a real peach.

"Hi, Jim," she said, taking off her wet jacket and scarf and dropping her shopping bag by the door.

"Hey, Beth's just getting ready, then we're going to catch a movie." He looked up from the magazine. "You can come too."

"Thanks but no thanks. I just downloaded a new Christmas romance I'm dying to read. You two have fun."

Her socked feet were slippery against the wide-planked, espresso-stained wood as she passed the kitchen and knocked on Beth's door. "Just me," she called in.

"What happened to 'see you in an hour'?" Beth met Grace's eyes in the mirror she was currently looking at to curl her hair. "I was about to call in the national guard."

"Why didn't we rent a basement apartment?" she asked, ignoring her friend's question.

"My mom was worried about mold and a cockroach invasion." She released a section of hair from the curling iron, and it fell in a perfect golden spiral against her head.

"Fair enough," she said, backing away from the door.

"Oh no you don't." Beth turned, one hand on her curling iron and the other beckoning her to come back. She sighed, ready to be patronized about going off with a strange man, or worse, get Beth rolling on happily-ever-afters, fairy tales, and wedding bells. The thing about a person in love was they wanted everyone else to feel the same way. Owen seemed great, but everyone was on their best behavior the first time they met someone, right? Well, not unhinge-your-jaw-and-begin-a-food-challenge-cheapskate Frank. He bit off more than he could chew the day he asked her out to dinner.

"What?" she asked in her most innocent voice, hand placed against the smooth edge of the door frame.

"You never answered my question." She honest to goodness clucked her tongue. "Oh," she groaned. "I'm my mother. How did this happen?"

"I really expected it to take longer. Like maybe when you hit forty-five or fifty, but you're already there, sister." She sighed and entered the room, flopping down on Beth's bed.

There was no escaping each other in an apartment this small anyway. Everything in Beth's room was a shade of pink. Light pink, pearl pink, hot pink. It was dizzying. Like a bottle of Pepto-Bismol—which she desperately needed after all that hot chocolate—had exploded and covered every surface. She hoped Jim was okay with pink, otherwise he was in for a life of misery. A pair of balled socks thumped into her shoulder.

"You know, that's the second thing you've thrown at me today." She tossed the socks back, hitting Beth in the rear. Served her right.

"That's what you get for agreeing that I've turned into my mother." She picked up another section of hair and wrapped it tightly around the scorching-hot iron. "So, spill. It's almost eight o'clock. Stores close at five thirty. You didn't drive your car, so where did you go?"

Beth would be both prison warden and mother if she someday had children. "Well, first there was this surly cashier, and toys were really cleared out, and then I bumped into this uncle."

"What was your uncle doing at a toy shop?" Beth raised a questioning brow to the mirror and released another curl over her shoulder.

"No, no. Not my uncle. An uncle. A cute one, looking for dolls for his nieces." That got Beth's attention, and she pulled the cord of her curling iron from the outlet and spun around to rest her hip on the dresser.

"So you met a cute uncle, and?" Her eyes widened, dreams of double dates dancing in her head, no doubt.

"I helped him find the dolls, and then he asked me to get

a hot chocolate with him." She scrunched her face waiting for one of Beth's patented over-the-top reactions. The long, drawn-out aww even brought Jim to the door.

"Everything okay in here?" he asked, looking from Beth to Grace then back again. "You're talking about me, aren't you?"

Beth giggled. "No, silly. I'll be out in two minutes tops." Jim shrugged and walked away in the direction of the living room.

"So you got hot chocolate, and?"

"I don't want to keep you from your date, but it was actually four hot chocolates and a cinnamon bun. It was the size of my head, and he didn't even blink when I ate my half and some of his." She got comfortable, leaning her forearms back against the pillows. Pink, of course.

"Call the justice of the peace. This is it. When are you seeing him next?" Beth asked, nearly bouncing out of her knee-high suede boots.

"Sunday." Nerves began to flutter around in her stomach like snowflakes. She didn't want to get her hopes up. It was okay to be single. It really was. Grace wanted to find someone special and eventually get married, but it didn't happen for everyone.

"Merry Christmas to you. Can't wait to meet him." Beth grabbed her purse and keys, looking as gorgeous as ever.

"You'll scare him off." She sat upright and crossed her arms over her chest.

"Okay, Miss *I leave my dirty laundry in heaps everywhere to trip Jim when he least expects it.*" Beth's hands went to her hips.

"Keeping him on his toes. But seriously, this guy—Owen—is kind of shy."

"So what?" She spritzed perfume in a mist in front of her and walked through it. "You're going to hide me under the bed until he pops the question?"

"I think you're getting a little ahead of yourself there. But hiding you under the bed might work out."

Beth rolled her eyes and marched through the threshold of her room. "What's his name so I can social media sleuth him during the movie credits?"

"I don't think he has Instagram or anything." She started to rearrange Beth's mountain of throw pillows that had toppled when she sat.

Beth's eyes narrowed. "This person doesn't sound like your type. At all."

She shrugged her shoulders, protectiveness over Owen surging through her. "Doesn't matter. I think that's why I like him."

"Wait up for me so we can talk about this when I get home, okay? I want to hear everything." She spun around, the heels of her boots clicking against the floor as she walked away.

"Yeah, sure," she muttered. A long yawn escaped her lips. No way was she waiting up for them. She picked up her phone and glanced at the screen, contemplated, and typed a text to Owen.

Did the abominable snowman eat you, or did you make it safely to your car?

LOL. The latter. See you Sunday.

After the sugar-coma heaven he'd given her this afternoon, she couldn't wait to see what their second date held.

But she pushed down the giddy feeling rising in her chest.

She couldn't get too excited about Owen being the person she'd glimpsed this afternoon. As long as she managed her expectations, she wouldn't get hurt.

Chapter Four

"On the second date of Christmas, a horse-drawn sleigh paired with soft snow showers set the tone for romance (so long as your date isn't allergic to horses)."
—The Twelve Dates of Christmas *by Paige Turner*

SATURDAY HAD ROLLED around, and Owen was no closer to figuring out a plan for Sunday that would top the hot chocolate tasting. His lack of creativity was making him dream up all sorts of worst-case scenarios, which was why he'd rummaged through his house looking for the romance novel his ex had chucked at him like a ninja star. He was going to do his best to show Grace a good time. Even if it meant reading *The Twelve Dates of Christmas* by Paige Turner.

"Okay, Paige. Help me out here." He tapped the book cover against his palm as he made his way back downstairs to the living room and flipped on the lights. He'd definitely need to take notes from the story. He studied the cover of a young couple clinking together mugs of what looked like hot cocoa. Well, at least he'd checked that off the list. He opened the book to the first chapter, smoothing the page flat, and started to read.

OWEN WOKE UP Sunday morning, still in the recliner. His glasses had slid over the tip of his nose, and the romance novel was open facedown over his leg. He must've taken a break from reading and dozed off. When *The Twelve Dates of Christmas* captured his attention, he'd been surprised. Fiction wasn't his normal genre, let alone romance. Something about the voice had drawn him in, and kept him reading until midnight. The story was about the hero and heroine redis-covering the magic of the holidays and falling in love over the course of twelve winter dates. The tone of the book was serious, but the little quips here and there had actually made him laugh. He took off his glasses and rubbed his eyes, before sliding them back on and picking up the notes he'd jotted down. It was a complete coincidence that they'd shared hot chocolate the first day they met.

Dates for Grace
1. ~~Hot cocoa at quaint café~~
2. Horse-drawn sleigh—ask Grace to lunch after? Check Yelp restaurant ratings.
3. European Christmas market
4. Glassblowing ornaments—dangerous???
5. Sledding
6. ~~Caroling~~ NOT A CHANCE
7. Baking and decorating cookies
8. Looking at neighborhood lights—not sure if Grace would like this.

9. *Roast marshmallows over fire outside—messy??*
10. ~~*Pillow fort, eggnog, holiday music, fire—*~~ *igloo + wine + stars?*
11. *Holiday movie marathon*
12. *Wreath-making class*

He rolled his shoulders, feeling more relaxed than he had the night before. Now that the book's hero had given him a guide for their first date, he could breathe easier—so long as he could pull it off before their agreed meet time of noon. He started a search on his phone for horse-drawn sleigh rides, made a call, and got lucky because someone had just canceled their reservation. After a long shower and a change of clothes, he was ready to pick up Grace.

WHEN OWEN PARALLEL parked in front of Grace's building, he spotted her through the entryway window. She straightened as she caught sight of him and stepped out of the building. The breath squeezed from his lungs. Her sable hair flowed around her shoulders in loose, glossy waves that caught the sunlight like reflective glass. She had on a different coat today, a burst of lemon that popped against the world of white. Indigo jeans hugged her legs up to the knees where they disappeared beneath shiny black boots. She smiled and waved, and he quickly jumped out of the driver's seat to open the passenger door. He grasped for the right words to say hello, to let her know how amazing she looked.

"You look like the sun." *No, no, no.* That came out all

wrong. He cringed at his blundered words. What he had meant was *You look like a ray of sunshine*, which now sounded pretty ridiculous too. He was weird. It was undeniable. He held the car door open, hoping she wouldn't turn on her heel and walk back into the building.

"Thanks." The silky notes in her voice made his heart pump to a new rhythm, as did the dazzling smile. "You too look like a round, burning ball of gas this fine afternoon," she said nonchalantly as she slipped inside the car.

He puffed his cheeks and blew out a long breath trying to regain some of his dignity as he rounded the car. Was he always this bizarre? And if so, how had he convinced women to date him in the past? He took a fortifying breath, ready to see this thing through even if it wounded his pride for all eternity, and got behind the wheel. He shifted into drive, pausing before leaving the parking space. "It's nuclear fusion. I mean, the sun isn't actually burning. Protons slam together emitting energy, which generates heat and…" *Couldn't just let it go, could you, Ellis?* He was blowing it. No romance novel could help him. "What I meant was you look beautiful, and the best thing about me blurting out peculiar statements is that you'll have fuel for those witty comments."

"This is true." She giggled, and the rock lodged at the base of his throat started to crumble away.

"Oh, I almost forgot." He wrapped his right hand around the cup of hot chocolate and held it out to her. "Peppermint bark."

He caught her smile widening from the corner of his eye before hearing a breathy sigh of appreciation after she took a sip. "Thank you." The surprise in her tone made him feel a foot taller. "But I wasn't really hurt the other day."

"My pride was hurt enough for both of us, so it's basically the same." He flipped on his directional and cautiously merged into traffic. It was taking all of his focus to keep his eyes on the road and not on the way Grace savored each sip of her drink, occasionally licking her lips or making a little sound of pleasure like she did at the café.

"We did get a pretty good laugh out of it though. My stomach ached so badly the other morning, my abs thought I'd been up all night training for a triathlon. Then they remembered who they belong to."

"Well, tell those nosy abdominal muscles to mind their own business, because today is for sleigh rides and lunch." He turned down a side road and spotted what looked to be an expansive barn.

"We're going on a sleigh ride?" Her suede-soft eyes widened, glinting with excitement. She turned to look out the side window, mouth gaping slightly as she took in the wide expanse of the countryside.

"You're not allergic to horses, are you?" His stomach dropped, and he jerked to the side to look at Grace.

"No. I am A-okay with horses. More than. This is amazing." She folded her hands in her lap and smiled. He liked how open and earnest her expressions were. That he didn't have to guess what she was feeling. Acres of gleaming snow bordered by soaring evergreens stretched across the countryside. The boughs of the trees were frosted in ice, and beyond them hovered the dips and rolls of the mountainside.

"Grace," he whispered, slowing the car. "Look out toward the tree line." She drew in a sharp breath. One that gave him an instant surge of pride for spotting the great big buck, stately and regal as he stood amid the snow and ice.

"I've never seen a deer this close, never mind antlers like that. Just wow." He slowly rolled past as the deer sprang into fluid motion, racing over the field. He said a silent thanks to Bambi. One point for wildlife.

He parked the car in front of a rustic-looking split rail fence. After patting his pockets to make sure he had his wallet and phone, he rounded to Grace's side of the car. She had already stepped out, smiling freely at him.

"Thanks again for the hot chocolate." She spun in a circle on her tiptoes. "This place is gorgeous. There's so much land." Her hair flew around her shoulders as she turned. "Shall we?" Palm up, she offered her gloved hand, and he locked his fingers with hers. Being with her was proving to be easier than expected. Conversation came effortlessly in the car, and it felt natural holding her hand—fantastic even.

They left a trail of footprints in their wake as they crunched through the snow to the carriage house.

"Owen, look!" She bounced on her toes and reached her right hand across her body to rest on his shoulder. The contact made his whole body buzz with pleasure at the simple touch. Her excitement would make riding in the questionably old sleigh for two worth it. It's not like they could operate the thing without safety checks. Right? He opened his mouth, then closed it to stifle the urge to ask if sleighs had seat belts. Strapped to the turn-of-the-century sleigh (*please let it be a good, sound replica*) was the equestrian version of Godzilla.

"What do you suppose they feed a horse of that size?"

The beast in question stomped its front feet impatiently and snorted, sending billows of steam out of nostrils as big as baseballs.

"Are you scared of horses?" She tilted her head to one side, amusement sparking in her gaze.

Terrified. He just hadn't realized it. Until now. "No, of course not. Who's scared of horses? Not me." The animal chose that exact moment to wrap its enormous, man-eating incisors around an apple its handler held out. Godzilla mowed the apple, snapping it down in seconds. Owen barely registered Grace tugging him along toward the sleigh. Her voice rose and fell in cheerful tones as she chatted up the driver. Godzilla twisted his head and stared him down, muscles bunching its shoulders and legs.

"Figgy will be pulling your sleigh today." The man's voice jolted him, and he refocused his attention, without turning his back to the horse.

"Who?" he asked, eyes darting from the horse to the man.

"Figgy Pudding is the horse's show name, but among friends we just go with the more casual Figgy."

He shared a sympathetic look with the horse. No wonder it had underlying rage issues with a name like that. "Okay. Figgy. That explains a lot." Grace nudged him, but the man continued to speak.

"I'm your coachman, Earl, and it's my pleasure to be the first to welcome you to Christmas at Emerson Farm." For the first time, Owen took in the man's top hat and long, black buttoned coat. He hoped Grace didn't mind the historical throwback. "Feel free to carol as we ride!"

Oh. Please. God. No.

"Aw. What do you think, Owen? Got a favorite Christmas jingle?" Grace must've sensed his discomfort because she grinned. She seemed to enjoy pushing him beyond his comfort zone.

"Please step up here." The coachman motioned toward the iron ledge hovering over the rails of the sled.

Grace got in first, and he tried to be a gentleman and not stare at her perfectly rounded backside. He slid in next to her, immediately scoping the area for seat belts. Nada. Earl popped up like a groundhog in the seat in front of them and snapped the reins. The sleigh jolted beneath him, and he wrapped his arm around Grace to keep her from falling forward. It took only a few moments for them to gain momentum, and they were gliding at a high rate of speed. The arctic wind sliced over their faces and tousled their hair. The scenery blurred past in a mist of green and blue and white.

"We're flying!" Grace yelled so she could be heard above the whoosh of wind and the bells clanking against Godzilla's harness (he was pretty sure the horse would appreciate Godzilla over Figgy). "I've always, always wanted to do this!"

And there it was. Every bit of apprehension dissolved at the joy brimming from her smile. He could do things that freaked him out a bit, so long as they weren't really dangerous like skydiving, hang gliding, free climbing. What was the worst that could happen on a tame sleigh ride? From up in the sleigh, he got a new appreciation for the horse pulling them. Its coat glistened silver, nearly as pure as the blanket of snow beneath its furry hooves.

"Me too." Instead of shouting the words, he leaned in closer to her ear.

"I have a feeling that's a stretch, but I'm having a great time." She looped her arm through his and leaned closer. "That's the most beautiful horse I've ever seen. Put a horn on his head and he'd be a unicorn."

"I'm sure Figgy would appreciate that just as much as his ridiculous name." The sleigh passed a gray stone gristmill with a navy-colored waterwheel. In the past, it would've harnessed power from the surrounding stream to grind wheat flour and cornmeal.

"Whoa," Earl called to the horse and it slowed to a halt. "My last patron lost a scarf, and I think I've spotted it. Hold tight." He slipped down from his post to retrieve the swatch of lavender fabric poking out from the snow.

"Does this thing have a parking brake?" he muttered to Grace, eliciting a chuckle.

"I think draft horses are really intelligent and responsive," Grace said, looking at the horse with wonder in her eyes. Maybe she was right. The driver had just bent down to retrieve the lost article of clothing when a sharp crack erupted to their left. They turned their attention to the direction of the noise, as a long branch weighed down by a thick glaze of icicles clattered to the ground right behind the horse's back legs. A panicked whinny sliced through the air, and Figgy bolted. The sleigh bumped wildly over the crests of snow, but it did nothing to slow the horse.

"Oh my gosh," Grace shrieked as the horse plowed over the landscape. Behind them the coachman was shouting and chasing the sleigh, but he was no match for the powerful beast at the helm of the iron deathtrap.

"What was that?" he yelled over the wind, heart flapping like a wounded bird. "Something about being responsive?"

"It's not his fault. He was spooked! We just need to grab the reins and try to slow him down." She jumped to the horse's defense and started to stand.

"No!" Manners fled and Owen grabbed Grace's arm above the elbow. "Sit on the floor in crash position."

"This isn't a jumbo jet."

How could she laugh at a time like this?

"You're right. It's worse. No airbags. No flotation device. No pilot! This whirlybird going down." He gave an exasperated huff when Grace gripped the seat in front of her, laughing in silent, shaking sobs.

When he looked up, his heart slammed into his throat, and he clutched the fabric seat with white knuckles. They were headed straight for the tree line.

Chapter Five

"Bravery takes many forms. (Unless there's a spider. Then all bets are off.)"
—The Twelve Dates of Christmas *by Paige Turner*

W HY WAS SHE laughing? Grace tried to get ahold of herself. This was kind of a sticky situation, but she tended to have inappropriate reactions to such things. Maybe it was her way of dealing with fear. Then Owen had used the word *whirlybird* and she'd just lost it. She wasn't even sure why she found it funny, probably because it sounded like something straight out of the forties. Now the horse was out of control, racing away from Earl and the stables at a break-neck speed. Wind ripped at her hair and tugged at her dangly earrings. She took a deep breath and gathered her composure. The sleigh was jolting in response to the rapid pace, making a disconcerting squealing sound as they went.

"I'm going to grab the reins," Owen shouted over the wind. "Hold on tight, just in case."

Grace struggled to catch her breath as Owen gripped the seat in front of them, hands colorless and trembling. Or was that the shaky movement of the sleigh? She squeezed her eyes shut, then peeked up again. He was climbing up and over, attempting to get closer to the reins. For someone who was nervous at the beginning of the sleigh ride, he was being incredibly brave. Her heart was walloping her ribs in quick blasts as Owen's hands closed over the reins.

"Easy," he said, and by some miracle the horse slowed to a walk. Plumes of condensation billowed from its nostrils. "Should we stop?"

"I think it's better to let him keep moving. Cool down a bit." She ignored her quivering limbs and clamored to the front. It was a lot harder to scale the seats then it looked, but she managed to slide onto the seat next to Owen.

"We did it." Owen shot her a heart-stopping smile, brimming with relief.

"You did it. You were amazing." She leaned in, giving him a soft shoulder bump. While she was panicking, he'd thought with a clear head and determined the best way to stop the horse. Her respect for him bumped up a notch, even though it was already pretty darn high. She held his steady gaze. Looking into his eyes was grounding after such an adrenaline rush. "Thank you." The words came out as a whisper and were almost lost against the blustery wind.

He smiled at her, then looked at the horse, eyes wide. "What's happening?" Alarm registered in his tone as the horse changed direction and stomped in a semicircle.

"Turning around, I guess." She shrugged. "He probably walks this trail often and knows the way back to the barn."

"Do we really want to put that much trust in the Stallion of Death?"

Grace chuckled. "He stopped very nicely when you got the reins." The horse plodded along, and for the first time, she really took in the countryside. The sky was a crisp, cloudless blue, and the rolling hills ahead glistened with yesterday's snow. Every breath was laced with fresh pine, Owen's subtle aftershave, and the earthy scents of hay from the horse.

"While Figgy's getting us back to point A, tell me about your favorite Christmas tradition," she asked, sinking back into the velvet upholstery.

Owen was quiet for a moment, then began to speak. "Well, my sister and I used to do this thing every year. My mom would make gingerbread and put toppings out. Frosting, gumdrops, all that kind of stuff. Then we'd have a gingerbread house building contest." A smile ghosted around his lips.

"Who won?" Holiday traditions were important, and she loved that Owen had some special memories tucked away. Her parents had made everything so magical, and someday she was going to do the same for her children.

"My parents judged the finished product on overall appearance and best structural design. They'd put the buildings through these tests to see how sturdy they were, and to see if the house was level." His smile widened. "Mom's an engineer too—retired now."

She clapped her hands together and grinned. "Sounds intense, and fun."

"It was. My sister usually won for the best-looking house. She just has this knack for decorating that the rest of us don't. My building was always a steel fortress though."

"Are you sure you didn't sneak some cement in with the sugar and flour?"

"Trade secret." He winked at her, inciting a flutter in her

belly. "And what about your best tradition?"

"That's a tough one, because I love all of them so much. Driving around looking at Christmas lights, decorating a big balsam fir and having that fresh forest scent hit you whenever you step into the house. Mostly, the time spent with my family. My parents got engaged on Christmas Eve, so my dad goes out of his way to make the season romantic for my mom. It's sweet—oh my gosh! Look. I think that's Earl up ahead." Since the horse calmed down, she'd been having a lot of fun talking to Owen. She didn't want to end yet, but she could see the top-hat clad man getting closer.

"Must be," he said, eyes squinting into the distance.

The man started to sprint when he caught sight of them. "Thank goodness! Are either of you hurt?" Earl slid to a halt, snow kicking up over his pants. He rested his hands on his knees, panting hard, chest heaving. It was still hard to believe the horse had been so spooked by the branch that it bolted off.

"I had one of the stable hands get some hot mulled cider going for you, and we have an outdoor hearth for when we cook with the camp kids. Had them fire it up so you can get warm. We are so sorry. This has never happened—"

"It's not anyone's fault." Grace offered Earl a smile, and his worried expression softened.

He stroked the horse's muzzle, then stepped back and gazed up at them. "I have a blanket tucked away in the front. I'll take my driver's seat back now, and you two can get warm." They made the switch, this time with a heavy blanket weighing comfortably over their legs, and were back on the trail in no time.

"Are you sure you're okay?" Owen's gaze roamed her face, as the wind rustled his hair. She snuggled into the downy blanket, but despite the added warmth, the adrenaline had chilled her skin. Warming up might take a bit of time.

"Thanks to you, yeah, I'm good. I could've done without the joyride, but I'm looking forward to telling the tale around the coffee machine at work tomorrow morning. And you know, the other women are going to be jealous that my date had the guts to climb over the seat of a moving sleigh to rescue me." She reached to the side, skimming his hand with her fingertips. "Thank you for getting us out of that situation." The bright sunlight bouncing off the snow did nothing to conceal Owen's discomfort at being thanked. She wasn't sure if it was a lack of experience with women or if it was the experiences themselves that made this gorgeous, intelligent man shy away from compliments and gratitude.

Yes, Owen had been scared out of his mind before the sleigh ride had even started, and that's why she was so impressed by his actions. He'd faced his fears and not only kept her safe, but the horse too.

"I'd appreciate if you left out that I'm still shaking, and needed to pry my fingers loose from the death grip I had on old Figgy's reins when Earl arrived." He rubbed the back of his neck and cleared his throat.

"Um, I think anyone would've been shaking. Do you hold yourself to inhuman standards, or did someone else?" Color flushed his cheeks. She should've waited to ask about his past, but her curiosity won.

"Well, I think I'm the one who tends to blunder things

up—with women mostly. Probably something I shouldn't tell the person I'm on a date with." His soft lips compressed into a thin grimace.

She scooted closer to him on the seat, so their outer legs were touching. A thrill tumbled through her at having him close. The fright they'd just experienced had brought them closer, and being snuggled beneath a cozy blanket together was intimate yet soothing. "Oh no, I definitely want to hear this."

A deep chuckle rose up from his chest, and she felt the vibrations to the soles of her feet. "I already brought you on Satan's stagecoach." He leaned in and whispered in her ear so Earl couldn't hear. "I don't think laying out my flaws will help me secure another date with you."

"I can't make any promises," she said, struggling to keep a straight face and failing. "But I'll be sure to take into consideration that you were the only thing separating me from broken bones this afternoon."

"That's really generous of you." The bemused grin and eye roll he cast her way made her feel light and relaxed all at the same time. He was opening up, getting comfier around her. "I've been told I don't possess a romantic bone in my body, even though I was being thoughtful—at least that's how I perceived it."

"Hmm…I'm going to need examples." As they crested the hill, a golden weather vane came into view, then the stables. If it weren't for the peeling paint chips on the clapboard siding and hunter green shutters, the structure would've been camouflaged by the snow. Sure enough, a small blaze was kindling in a stone hearth bordered by two stone slabs for sitting. The sleigh bypassed the barn and continued to the spot that had the fire crackling. Two stable hands rushed up to the sleigh, helped them down, and whisked them to one of the benches. She sank down, shivering as the flames licking the walls of the hearth thawed her. *Oh!* The seats were naturally heated by the hearth, and it was magical. After pouring them mugs of cider, the employees left the thermos in the snow at their feet.

"That was a whirlwind," she said, looking around to make sure they were alone. Owen snorted in agreement.

"Would you still like to go to lunch after we finish up this cider?"

"My favorite part of the day." She grinned at him, and was happy when his own dimpled smile appeared. "But while we're drinking this, I'd love to hear those examples." She eyed him over the rim of her glass, fragrant steam rising up to tickle her nose.

"Maybe we should talk about something else." His face flushed a bit, but he didn't look too embarrassed, so she pushed.

"Isn't it only fair that I know exactly what I'm getting into?" She had to bite her lip to keep from giggling, but she did grin so he knew she was being playful. Why would it matter to her what other women thought? She'd only been out with him twice, and she could already tell he was a great guy. Their loss was her win. When she was younger—around the time she wrote *The Twelve Dates of Christmas*—her idea of a relationship was being swept away by over-the-top dates. Now if she read the book, it would exhaust her just thinking about it—not to mention embarrass the heck out of her.

She'd been so immature, it was cringe-worthy. Now, five years later, the perfect guy would be someone she could be herself around, someone she could kick back with after a long workday wearing fuzzy sweatpants and her hair in a knot on top of her head. Someone she could trust, respect, and enjoy spending time with.

Owen rubbed at his ear and shifted against the stone bench. "I guess that is logical, even though I having a feeling you're duping me here."

She crossed her heart. "No. I promise I won't judge."

"Well, my last girlfriend would complain that I didn't make her feel special, but I would try to go out of my way to do just that." The corners of his lips dipped into a frown.

"How?" Maybe if she could help him figure out what went wrong, he'd have more confidence. It wasn't like she wanted him wooing other women, but he did deserve to feel self-assured. A spark of something ugly, something a lot like jealousy, pricked her. Seemed her mind was already made up about seeing Owen again. She *liked* him. She dated now and then but never got the sense of that special sparkle. Having that feeling so soon with Owen made her a bit off-kilter and unsettled.

"Like take her car for an oil change." He pushed his glasses up his nose and focused in on her again. "Or schedule regular updates on her computer so it would have the latest technology features or make her lighting more energy efficient."

Don't laugh. Don't laugh. Her cheeks puffed. She desperately tried to hold the cider in her mouth.

"Who doesn't want energy efficiency?" he said, thrusting

back his shoulders and pulling in a deep breath.

That was it. The drink sprayed out of her mouth and she clapped a hand over her lips. *Utter mortification.* "Oh my God, I'm sorry. I did not mean to shower you."

Grace didn't get embarrassed often, but now was one of those rare moments. It was bad enough that she had laughed when she promised no judgment, but she'd spit on him like a grouchy camel. Owen took off his splotchy glasses and wiped them in circular motions over the hem of his shirt.

"Not exactly the reaction I was looking for," he said, slipping his now-dry specs back on.

"I wasn't laughing at you. Okay, I was, but only because I could picture you doing all those things, and it was really sweet and yes, also funny because your love language was probably very different from your ex-girlfriend's."

Owen's face twisted, brows pulling together. "Love language?"

"Yeah, like maybe her idea of romance was sweet words or flowers and yours was fixing something to make life easier for her. You know, acts of service. Small things that often go unnoticed but are really missed when they're not there anymore. Casanovas are a dime a dozen, but a hybrid energy conservationist/personal digital firewall/maintainer of mechanical maintenance? Now that is rare." She smiled, looking up at him from under her lashes.

"Stop it." He crossed his arms over his chest, but from the way he was smiling, she could tell he was trying not to laugh.

"No seriously. Flowers wilt after a few days, but computer updates are the gift that keep on giving." She inched her hand closer to his.

"What's your love language? You know, aside from driving a taco truck up to your curb."

She laughed, liking that he'd remembered her favorite meme about the food truck. "I do like spontaneous surprises, but that's not all that is important. I'd like a partner, someone I can rely on when things don't go as planned. Anyone can get along when the sun's shining, finances are good, but throw in a leaky faucet and some unexpected bills. If you get along then, that's the real deal." Grace looked along the line of her shoulder at the fire.

A few years ago, she wouldn't have thought what Owen said was romantic at all. Now? Having someone who cared enough to ensure that even your computer was running like a high-performance machine sounded incredible. It might not be like receiving jewelry or visiting a candlelit restaurant, but it was those small gestures that made the difference in a real relationship.

"And you know, the impromptu hot chocolate tasting and this sleigh ride were both really thoughtful, and romantic too. Maybe the girls you were dating didn't see it, or weren't at the point in their lives when they were ready to."

Owen's movement captured her attention. He slid his hand across the bench, capturing her own, and swiped his thumb over her knuckles. The pad of his finger was a cashmere-soft whisper, infused with warmth and begging her to get cozy. His eyes dropped to her lips, as a lick of light from the hearth hollowed his cheek and accentuated his thickly lashed lids. His gaze returned, locking her in place with its intensity. Was Owen going to make the first move and kiss her? Anticipation steeled her for the moment, keeping her perfectly still aside from the tiny snowflakes whirring in her stomach.

Owen was going to kiss her, and she was going to let him. She was light-headed, body humming with anticipation, as he leaned closer, enough to catch the clean notes of his aftershave. The crunch of feet behind them barely registered. It must have for Owen though, because he pulled back, desire and regret storming over his features. He gave her hand a squeeze as Earl walked over to check on them.

She might've been happy to see him running down the trail an hour ago, but right now? Not so much.

Chapter Six

"On the third date of Christmas, tiny firefly lights lit a path through the Christmas market, the scent of Bavarian apple strudel hung in the air, swirling with good cheer and open hearts. (Did I mention Bavarian apple strudel?)"
—The Twelve Dates of Christmas *by Paige Turner*

OWEN'S WORK WEEK had been inhumanly long. He was picking up Grace tonight, and like every time her name played through his mind, flurries of anticipation tingled over his body. He'd almost kissed her by the fireside last weekend. The mere touch of her skin alone left him breathless. Remembering the time and place, he'd reluctantly stopped himself, but disappointment had flashed in her eyes. *Wishful thinking most likely.* He glanced around his foyer and patted his pockets. *Keys, wallet, phone.* He checked off the essential items in his head, and stepped outside. The frigid air slammed into the back of his throat as he breathed in, then quickly released it. A wall of condensation materialized in front of him. The entryway spotlight illuminated the snow-covered stone steps and walkway as he treaded to the car. His backside hit the seat of the defrosted vehicle, just as the hands-free calling system lit up the dashboard. He loved his sister, but her timing was garbage.

"Hey." He glanced at the backup camera as he reversed down the long driveway, automatic headlights and taillights shining spotlights on the snow.

"Is my baby brother ready for his big date?" Sage had always loved to tease and harass him, but the moment someone else tried to do the same, they were a goner. Sage took her role of older sister very seriously.

"Please." He groaned and slowed to a stop before backing onto the main road.

"So where are you taking her? Are you still following the book?" Excitement was a palpable beat in her voice. It wasn't really romantic that he had to gain date inspiration from a story, but he liked Grace. He'd researched the book, and it was a best seller so it must be what women wanted, fantasized about having. All week he'd squirreled the novel away in his desk drawer, reading small snippets during his lunch break.

"Maybe. If she's into the idea. I thought it would be hard to find a European-inspired Christmas market, but there's one in the next town." He glanced in his side mirror, turned on the directional, and took a left toward Grace's apartment.

"That does sound nice. Grab her a trinket there. It will make her think of you. Oh, and don't forget you volunteered to babysit tomorrow. So don't stay out all night."

They said their goodbyes and ended the call just as he arrived at Grace's place. She was standing on the corner, bathed in light from the lamppost above. Her hair was down again, rolling over her shoulders and arms, bouncing with a life of its own as she moved toward the car. She waved, opened the door, and slid inside.

"Hey, you." She grinned, flashing her snow-white teeth at him. He decided right then that he was a teeth guy. Something red and glittery caught his eye between her curls, and curiosity made him forget manners. Before he could register his actions, his fingers were skimming along the satin strands. He wanted more. To test the weight of it in his hands, to tangle his fingers up in it. Instead he plucked the stray scrap of ribbon from the glossy mass and held it up.

"Two-timing with one of Santa's helpers?" He wiggled the string, and she tugged it away.

"Only on weekdays." She smiled. He was starting to anticipate the way her lips curved, the grooves that defined the apples of her cheeks, how the corners of her eyes crinkled ever so slightly. There was an empty, fluttery pain in his stomach. *You don't fall for someone on the third date.* Warmth seeped through his chest like a tumbled mug of cider. Logically, he knew it was simply nature's cocktail of serotonin, dopamine, and endorphins pumping into his bloodstream, shaken not stirred by Grace and the way she was looking at him right now. Smiling like that.

"If you really must know, wrapping makes me incredibly stressed. I always end up the losing party in the fight against Scotch tape. The way it curls up or gets a piece of hair stuck in it making it unusable, because then people will know I don't vacuum." Her smile faded, and she turned to him with a serious expression. "You're a clean freak. Tell me you keep your house as neat as a dumpster fire in June or this thing is totally not going to work."

"Sorry," he said, staring at the road, trying to keep a

straight face. "I'm basically the love child of Lysol and bleach."

"I knew there had to be something." She craned against the headrest in a dramatic fashion that made him smile wider. Grace was silly, and it was adorable. So many people took life so seriously. He took life seriously. Grace took everything in stride from what he'd seen so far. And everything he'd seen about her, he liked.

"Should I let you off here, then?" He slowed the car, enjoying being silly right along with her. Something he didn't do very often. "Or would you like to continue on to the Christmas market?"

Her eyes widened, mouth dropping into a little O. Either he'd offended her or the idea of holiday shopping was incredibly appealing to the opposite sex, just like Paige Turner had predicted.

"I really shouldn't have to answer that. I retract my earlier statement. I'm just fine with tidy. Tidy is good." She was still relaxed, leaning back in the seat when she angled her face toward him. Her hair was caressing her cheek, draping over the front of her coat. Her delicious lava-cake eyes were warming him from the inside out. He nearly drove off the road.

"So long as you're not the one cleaning?" He raised one brow, not daring to look at her sultry features again. At least while operating heavy machinery.

"You catch on fast." The laugh was audible in her tone, good-natured and approachable. Something that helped his comfort level with Grace immensely. If she was angry or upset or slighted, her eyes and voice would be a dead giveaway. "I guess we might have to test that opposites theory."

Some people said opposites attract, but how did that work out long-term when one wanted to backpack through Europe and the other wanted to spend a peaceful summer reading on the shores of Nantucket? Or when one wanted spicy Punjabi cuisine that wreaked havoc on the other's stomach? *Stop.* They'd been on two and a quarter dates. He had the tendency to analyze the likelihood of a positive outcome before he got involved, but Grace made him want to bury his typical caution in the snow. Maybe it was the way she didn't take herself too seriously, or her sarcastic humor. Maybe it was that instant zap of chemistry, one he thought only simmered between the pages of books or on movie screens. Whatever it was, he hadn't experienced the blinding burst of attraction that he'd felt with Grace. It was something that made him pause. She was someone he could easily begin to really like, but he'd been wrong in the past.

"I'm excited. I've always wanted to go to the European-inspired markets nearby, but I've never had a chance. Oh," Grace gave an appreciative sigh as they pulled in the parking lot. "Look, how pretty."

Up ahead, a quaint winter wonderland had been erected in an outdoor park. Tiny fairy lights swooped in golden slopes over handcrafted wooden stalls. He turned off the engine and rounded the car for Grace, holding out his hand to help her out of the car. She stood up, gloved palm in his, and gasped as she slid on the slick pavement directly into him. Their bodies smacked together, and he quickly steadied her. The scent of her shampoo, a burst of cherry and plum, tantalized the air, overriding all his other senses. The press of her hands against his shoulders awakened his skin, suddenly electrified by her touch. Beneath his jacket, the fine little hairs on his arms and neck stood, and gooseflesh puckered down the length of his arms. His hands were planted on her hips—a feminine flair of curves, which every cell in his body instantly responded to in a needy, unsettled way.

"Are you okay?" He cringed at the sound of his voice, a low-pitched growl that belonged to someone else.

"I'm good." She stepped back, but only after a moment of hesitation. Did she feel it too? Because his eyes were about to roll back in his head from the close contact. She slipped her arm through his, and they began to crunch through a new layer of fresh snow. Grace tilted her head and sniffed the air, drawing in a long, satisfied breath.

"Sugared pecans, wood smoke, and cinnamon. I can't think of a better smell," she sighed.

"I can," he murmured, still imagining burying his face in her hair. They entered the market, a hazy glow of movement, light, and color.

"What's that?" Her brows were raised, but she was taking in all the new sights and sounds, which was good because he hadn't realized he'd spoken the words aloud.

"Hmm? Oh, nothing." He shrugged and released the breath he was holding. Just because he'd given up on being smooth didn't mean he wanted to embarrass himself in front of her. Grace was still captivated with the festive marketplace around her though, and didn't ask him again.

The atmosphere was different from anything he'd experienced before, kind of like Grace. *Thanks, Paige Turner.* A light snowfall drifted over the wooden stalls where vendors sold their merchandise and crafts. Mulled cider was being poured from several stands, and notes of sweet red apples, clove, and orange hung in the air. Displays were bursting with treats, which he considered a big score. Grace had a sweet tooth, and he would love to buy her a little something.

"Before we go any farther, how about a drink and a pastry?" He lifted his chin toward the nearest cider cart. "Kind of seems to be our thing." His heart was pumping in double time with her smiles, her nearness.

"You know, I think it is."

They went to the first lineless cart, ordered drinks and something that looked a lot like fruit cake. Warmth from the to-go cups permeated through his gloves, and he turned to hold one out to Grace. She stepped close and took the drink from his hands. They shared their first sip, eyes locked as snow spun in the air around them. Her pupils dilated as she watched him, onyx spreading over gold. Suddenly he didn't want the drink, because if the cup was in his hands, he couldn't be touching her. Brushing the snowflakes from the tips of her hair, pushing the soft spirals over her shoulders.

They chose a bench and sat to share the not-really-fruitcake. "Are there nuts in that too?" He'd always had a very simple palate.

Grace simply chuckled. "It's called stollen, and yes there's fruit and nuts, but I promise it will be like nothing you've ever tried."

She broke off a piece and held it up to his mouth. The cake looked much more appealing from this angle, but only because it was between her pink-polished fingers.

He bit off a small bite of the cake, intending to choke it

down. He didn't have to. The powdered sugar topping melted against his tongue, leading the way for the rich, aromatic cake.

"That's good." He never would've tried that under normal circumstances, but now he was glad, and not just because Grace was beaming at him with a satisfied expression. They split the remaining cake, each periodically stopping to brush the sugar from their coats.

"Ready?" she asked when they'd finished, holding out her hand to him.

They skirted through the crowds, walking hip to hip.

"You got your nieces gifts," she said, linking her hand with his. "Who else is on your Christmas list?"

"My sister, Sage, and my parents. What about you?" He couldn't help looking at her wide-eyed wonder as she took everything in.

"Nora is done, and as always, I went a little overboard on toys. In my defense though, I do only have one sister. I haven't gotten my dad anything yet, or Beth. Visiting a Christmas market was on our to-do list, but we're both busy with work, and then Beth got a boyfriend," she said with shrug.

"This is a first for both of us then." They lifted their arms, creating a bridge as they walked on either side of a wicker deer with a checkered ribbon bow.

"I'm happy we get to share it." If her voice was a fraction softer, her words would've been lost among the chatter and music. Her admission made him feel ten feet tall.

"Me too," he murmured.

Grace slid to a stop at one of the vendor stalls. "Oh, look

at these!" She leaned in to get a closer look at the rows of nutcrackers, brightly painted like toy soldiers in glossy shades of scarlet and cobalt. She chose one with a fuzzy gray beard. "These are too cute. It's just the thing to brighten up Beth's desk at work." She ended up buying more than one before they moved onto the next cart.

He laughed at the wooden toys at the next stall. "Grace, look at these." She sidled up to the cart to look over the merchandise. The glorious scent of her hair was still detectable, even with the competing fragrances peppering the air. "My dad would get a kick out of this." He picked up a carving of a man holding a big pair of spectacles and a Snellen eye chart with capital letters ranging from big to small.

"I love the mustache and the puffed hair at the temples. I'm guessing your father is an optometrist?" She looked up at him, cheeks rosy, smile bright.

"He is." If there was a time he'd been more comfortable with a woman, just walking and talking, having a nice time, he couldn't recall it. Shopping had never been one of his preferred pastimes, but strolling around looking at things people created with their own hands was fun.

Grace bought Beth nesting dolls painted like owls from an artist who handcrafted them in all varieties, while he got his mom and sister homemade candles and decorative holders. Baubles, ornaments, Christmas cards, and expertly crafted toys were on display, beckoning patrons to stop and make a purchase. Grace lingered over a plump porcelain kitten tangled up in a colorful strand of lights, and when she was busy paying for another item, he snuck away to get it for her.

"I could spend hours here," she said, bags dangling from each arm.

They'd walked to the center of the market, where a towering balsam fir decorated in festive ornaments was the focal point. The lights sprinkled over the tree reflected in Grace's dark hair, as she looked up at him with an open, inviting expression that made his heart stumble.

"Because of the company, right?" He leaned down and gave her a soft shoulder bump, stepping in closer beside her.

"That might have something to do with it." The low purr of words stripped his breath, flooding him with warmth in place of oxygen. A slow smile bloomed over her face, blinding him to everything else but her.

"Yeah?" he choked out, pulse throbbing beneath his skin.

"Yeah." She leaned her head on his shoulder as they looked at the lights, and the fuzzy ball on the tip of her hat tickled his cheek. "Thanks for bringing me here. I think I'm still in awe."

Needing her closer, he took a chance and wrapped his arm around her shoulders. "I am too." A sense of calm settled over him, even as his nerve endings snapped into overdrive. The weight of her head pressing into his coat, the strands of her hair tickling his chin, the way the outside of her hip pressed into his.

"I didn't know you had such a passion for holiday shopping." With all the glittering lights surrounding them, Christmas music piping through hidden speakers, and magical scents drifting through the air, the sensory experience that struck him the most was Grace. Just Grace.

"Not the shopping." The air between them grew thick, so much that he had difficulty drawing a breath after those words. Honest. Maybe he was being too honest. Opening himself up for hurt or letting her see too much of what he was feeling. He didn't want to scare her off, but there wasn't a trace of hesitation in her eyes.

"You have a snowflake on your cheek." He skimmed his fingers over her soft skin, brushing it away.

Grace's tawny irises turned to a rich brown, soft as suede, sparking with something that looked a lot like intrigue and perhaps something more. They were huddled close, energy swarming between them like the snowfall. His heart ricocheted against his ribs once, then twice, losing time and place in the moment between them.

Her eyes dropped to his lips, then back up again. He was starting to feel like someone might've spiked his cider, a bit woozy and disoriented. Once he kissed Grace, he had a feeling nothing would be the same again. Things were going so well… If he kissed her and she didn't feel a spark, his time with her would be over. She was worth waiting for. He cleared his throat and straightened just as shouting broke out around them. Three teenagers dashed past, circling the massive tree. Another reminder that they weren't completely alone out here, and now wasn't the right time to kiss Grace. He wanted to get to know her better before they took a physical step in their relationship. She looked to the side and tucked her hair neatly behind her ears, a blush darkening her cheeks.

Chapter Seven

*"To kiss, or not to kiss? (Hint: before you seek out the
mistletoe, snack on a candy cane for minty-
fresh breath.)"*
—The Twelve Dates of Christmas *by Paige Turner*

*H*OLY SMOKES. OWEN had almost kissed her—again.
Then he didn't. What the heck? If the power-driven
charge in the air wasn't a telltale sign, his swollen pupils and
the rapid pulse visible at the base of his jaw certainly were.
He'd been in the moment, just like her, until his focus had
drifted, eyes glossing over like he was weighing the pros and
cons. Heat spiked up her cheeks. *Ugh.* She hated blushing,
but geez, she'd been all puckered up. For a moment she felt
like the heroine of her own love story. Now she was wondering if she'd done something wrong—another thing she
disliked. *It's not always about you.*

Something groused in the back of her mind. Her spine
stiffened, a red flag rising to half-mast. Why hadn't she seen
it before now?

"You okay?" Owen leaned back to search her face. A
sharp pain pinched the inside of her cheek, and she realized
she was gnawing at it with her teeth.

Hot cocoa. A horse-drawn sleigh. The Christmas market. All scenes from *The Twelve Dates of Christmas.* It had to be a coincidence that their dates were mirroring the scenes out of the book she'd written under the guise of Paige Turner, the pen name she'd created with a good chuckle and an eye roll from Beth.

Beth.

She had to talk this out with her and get her take on the similarities. Maybe she was being silly. All the things she wrote about could be considered common winter dates, right? And if he had read the book, had he somehow sought her out despite her pseudonym and lack of a photograph on the back cover? No, it didn't make any sense. Overreacting was something she prided herself on not doing, preferring to project calm while internally freaking out.

"Grace?" His hand was stroking the length of her hair, and the instant need to lean into his touch was there, right beneath the surface. She'd never depended on anyone but her parents and Beth. She just hadn't had that kind of relationship with a man before. Owen was the type of guy you could lean on, but she wasn't about to cast away her independence. A relationship was something she'd always put off for her career. She wasn't looking for serious, but serious was staring her right in the face with worried green eyes and a soft expression. Her stomach flip-flopped. The last thing she wanted to do was lead Owen on when she wasn't sure what she wanted, or risk her perfectly intact heart. Her mother would look at her with a healthy dose of disappointment if she'd known Grace's train of thought. *Without risk, there's no reward.*

"Sorry…I just drifted." She hoped that was enough to

convince him nothing was really wrong, because it wasn't. *Well, maybe.* The material of his jacket skimmed along her fingers as she brushed away a stray snowflake.

"Are you sure that's it?" He tilted his head, the lights from the tree brightening his close-cut chestnut hair to a burnished gold.

"Yeah." She tucked her hands into her jacket as a gust spun around them. "Christmas tends to occupy a big space in my brain."

"Well, you have the slime beasts for Nora, and it looks like you've made a dent in the shopping list for your family, and possibly the entire town." He gave her overstuffed shopping bag a pointed glance.

"I'm not the only one who went overboard." She couldn't resist leaning in to give him a playful shoulder bump. Maybe she was being silly. There's no way he could know she'd written the book.

"Your love of shopping is infectious." They both surveyed the bags in their arms.

"Treasure hunting, you mean." She tilted her head and grinned, liking the way his hair was currently puffing up at the top, like he was the conductor for the electrical wave pulsing between them. "Shopping is what you do at a mall or a big box store. All of this?" She waved a hand over their purchases. "It's made with love, something you can't just pop into any retailer and find."

"Well, in that case, there might be a treasure for you in one of these bags. Want to go sit?" Owen gestured to one of the vacant wrought-iron benches near the tree.

"Sure." Her voice was nonchalant, but inside she was

anything but. Owen had bought her something? Did he notice that she'd picked out something for him while his back was turned? It was just a silly little thing, but it made her think of their first official date.

They crossed to the bench and sat, and Owen turned to rummage through one of his parcels, glasses slipping down over his nose before he shoved them back into place. She stole a long look at him, the guy who had just incited a cerebral traffic jam in her mind with that almost-kiss. When Owen turned back to her, his typically open expression was guarded. He swallowed hard, throat bobbing with the motion. In his hand was a gift-wrapped box tied in scarlet and gold ribbon.

"It's not even Christmas." She tugged at her scarf, suddenly too snug around her neck. Owen was waiting for her to take the gift. Watching for her reaction. Opening presents was an oddly intimate act. Maybe it was always being coached by parents to say thank you, fearful of letting your smile slip at the wrong moment, knowing someone was anticipating how you'd receive what they'd given.

"It's not a Christmas gift," he said, moving a piece of her hair behind her shoulder. The casual touches he'd been giving her all evening, a lingering shoulder bump, his fingers laced with hers, gave them a deeper level of connection. She'd be lying if she said being closer to him on a physical and emotional level didn't fill her with a joyful buzz.

"What kind then?" The ribbon was sheer against the pads of her fingers, giving way with an easy tug. She crossed her legs, letting the trim fall neatly along the seam of her legs.

"The just-because kind." A small smile flitted over his lips, and she could see her reflection and the light snowfall in his eyes.

"You know, that's rumored to be the best kind." Her heart was beating double time. She slid her fingers beneath the fold in the paper, popping apart the tape with a quick snap.

"I'll let you be the judge." He shifted on the bench, closing the gap between them.

The paper fell away, and beneath the lid of the cardboard box was the mischievous kitten she couldn't justify buying for herself at the market. She hadn't looked at it long, and made no mention of liking or wanting it, and yet, Owen had read her correctly. For the past two years, she'd casually dated, but so far the soul-deep connection was seriously lacking…and then there was Owen.

"The verdict is in. I'm voting in favor of the plaintiff." She traced the feline's sculpted fur, cool and hard to the touch. The orange tabby was wrapped in a net of lights, but looked rather pleased at his predicament. "This is really special. Thanks." She held his stare for a moment, smiling, then placed it back inside the protection of the box, closing the top.

"Does that mean I get another date?" He gave her a skewed grin, the one that pronounced his dimples the most and did something erratic to her vitals.

"Are you bribing the court?" She pressed her hand to her chest and leaned forward, grinning. Her knee bumped his, but she didn't bother to scoot back.

"I guess it depends on the answer." The snow began to

pick up, circling them in a curtain of silver. The light and movement from the market faded away, leaving them secluded. Warmth expanded in her stomach. She could vividly imagine how his lips would feel against hers.

"I'd really like that. I don't want you to feel as though you have to plan something to entertain me though. I mean, the sleigh ride, all this." She swept her hand in a circular motion, gesturing to the market. "It's been amazing, but I'm happy to just hang out too." She cleared her throat, not missing the way his brows crinkled in the center, as if he was trying to decide if she was serious about spending some low-key time together. "I, ah, actually saw something I wanted to give you too." She tucked her hair hastily behind her ear and handed him the brown bag from one of the market stands.

"You didn't have to do that," he said, holding the package with both hands like it was something precious.

"I wanted to, but really, it's silly." The tips of her ears burned as he unfolded the plain tissue paper and held up the wooden spring toy.

His brows lifted, eyes dancing with delight above raised cheeks. "This is awesome." He sat up straighter and pulled at the elastic string. The horse bounced and swayed. "It's Figgy Pudding. Thank you." He draped his arm around her shoulders and gave a squeeze. "It will have a place of honor at my work desk, and when I'm stressed out and look at it, I'll think of you."

There was a newfound lightness in her limbs. One that came from making someone else smile. She'd happily put that look on his face a million times over.

The snow picked up as they sat there, but she was warm

in the crook of Owen's arm, too content to move. "It's like someone tipped a snow globe upside down," she murmured. Was it the wonder of Christmastime coaxing these new emotions out of hiding? Ones that made her completely aware of the rhythm of her heart when she was in Owen's presence. Ones that turned her skin into a translucent sheath, so even featherlight touches felt like smoldering embers scattered along the surface. Beth had caught her humming—*humming*! Would this all disappear along with the holiday radio station after New Year's or did Owen really have keeper stamped all over him?

"I like being trapped in the same snow globe." Owen grinned with the same pleased expression as the cat statue tucked away in its box. She liked it too, but she was hesitant to admit it. This thing growing between them was so new to her, fragile like a snow globe. She was fearful that one wrong move would shatter what they were building, and the direction they were moving would be lost. She'd never settled, secretly holding out for the weak-in-the-knees, sweaty-palm, swoony feeling. Grace had just about given up hope that she'd find something as magical as her parents had. Until now.

PAJAMA-CLAD AND WITH red wine in hand, Grace and Beth sat on the sofa in their apartment. Grace leaned into the arm, sinking down into the cushions. The unicorn horn from the top of her silly onesie was starting to sag, bobbing in front of her eyes.

"Please put the cat down and listen." Grace blew out a long breath through pursed, impatient lips as Beth picked up the porcelain kitten for the third time.

"It's just so sweet. I'm sorry, but watching you date has been like witnessing a cliff-jump belly flop in slow motion. Half the time I don't even want to peek. This guy is nice." She placed the figurine next to the uncorked, almost depleted bottle of wine.

"If you have to say 'I'm sorry' before something, it's generally rude." Grace took a sip of cabernet, bold and dry along her tongue. "Unfortunately, what you say is also true. Don't you think it's weird at all though? The dates have been completely similar to the book." She inspected her glass, as though it held all the answers to her questions.

Beth huffed, a strand of hair floating up with her exhale. "I think in typical Grace fashion, you're looking for something that might not exist." The pillows piled around Beth were all different colors, making it look like she was tucked into a rainbow cocoon.

"Seriously?" She shifted to catch the throw blanket before it slipped to the floor. "You're the one who always says we're practically twins." She wound the blanket around her shoulders, fighting the shivers that kept shaking through her. The old building was drafty, and the thought of Owen reading her book unsettled her. Maybe the dates had nothing to do with the book, but if they did, how did she tell him she'd written it? She'd been a different person then— younger, different priorities, less life perspective. What if he thought she wanted him to plan something big each time they went out? It wasn't up to him to keep things fun. Not to mention that was a lot of pressure for anyone.

"Well, yeah. Except I'm the sweeter, more congenial twin." Beth shrugged, a smirk curving along her lips.

"Really? I'd love to know which planet that's on." She muffled her laugh against the rim of her glass, accidently clinking it against her upper tooth.

"Gracie, I'm just saying you can be a tough nut to crack." Beth held up her hands, then ducked when Grace tossed a sequined throw pillow at her. "Besides, I don't recall your hero setting up a hot cocoa tasting on the fly."

"But they did have hot chocolate." The wine was making her fuzzy and warm, kind of like being with Owen. *Oh, she was in so much trouble.* The cinnamon candle flickering on the coffee table puffed sweet, spiced scents into the air. The fragrance brought her right back to the Christmas market where she'd been two hours earlier. Maybe she'd forever associate some of her favorite holiday things with Owen.

Beth placed her wine beside her on the table, wrapped a fleece blanket around her shoulders, then picked up her drink by the stem. "Christmastime is joined at the hip with hot chocolate, sleigh rides, and Christmas markets. If he takes you to make ornaments, then we'll talk." Beth eyed her over her rapidly draining glass.

"So, what about Jim? Does your brother know you're seeing him yet?" Her eyelids were suddenly weighted, and she rested the side of her head against the back of the couch.

"Not yet." Beth pulled in the left side of her cheek, her tell of really mulling something over. "I didn't want to share until things got serious."

"Because you figured it wouldn't work out?" Gosh, they

really were like a pair of pessimistic twins.

"Exactly." Beth stretched out farther on the couch, her cat slippers poking out from beneath her blanket. They seriously had all the makings of single, middle-aged stereotypes.

"Hmm…in typical Beth fashion," she said, throwing her friend's words right back.

Beth rolled her eyes, and they both laughed into their empty glasses. After a few moments, her phone pinged. She and Beth shared a wide-eyed glance.

"It's Owen, isn't it? Please say it is." Beth swung her legs over the side of the couch, just enough to lean in and grab the tray of macrobiotic wheatgrass and kale cookies her mother had delivered to their doorstep. What was a cookie without sugar? Or frosting?

"Want?" Beth held out the plate, and Grace wrinkled her nose, holding up her hands to ward her off. Cookies weren't supposed to smell like garlic…and canned soup.

"They're green, and it's not because of food coloring." Grace ducked into the collar of her onesie like a turtle. The candle had done wonders for the smells emanating from the cookies, but nothing would help with them so close to her nose.

Beth shrugged and slid the tray back on the table. "I'm pretending it's chocolate chip." She took a bite, then grimaced.

"Not sure your imagination can stretch that far." She chuckled as Beth held her nose to swallow the tiny bite.

"Mmh. No, me neither," she said, shaking her head. "So read it already!" Beth repositioned, standing on her knees to lean closer to the phone Grace was currently shielding with the curve of her hand.

"He wants to know what I'm doing next Saturday." She'd never gotten giddy over someone's text messages before.

"Well?" Beth nudged her way closer, trying to peek.

"I can't exactly type with you hovering." Grace twisted on her side, sitting upright to respond to the message away from too-curious eyes.

Beth flopped down on the couch, the cushions giving a light bounce with the movement. "You'd never speak to me again if I let you screw this thing up."

"I think I can manage one text, thank you," she said, rolling her eyes. "I'll ask him if he wants to hang here," she mumbled more to herself than her friend. She typed in the message, pressed send, and placed the phone on the coffee table. It wasn't like she was waiting on the edge of her seat to see how he responded. *Liar, liar, pants on fire.* But she had to show some restraint, or she'd not only look desperate, she'd feel like it too. After a minute or so went by, she tucked her feet beneath her on the couch, getting cozy again.

Beth wiggled her brows, and she wasn't even annoyed. Instead she just smiled and rested her head against a throw pillow. The timed lights in the kitchen had snapped off, leaving the twinkling garlands framing their picture window as a light source. It was late. Time to go to bed.

"Night." She stretched her arms up, leaning toward the left and right. The strain of stiff muscles along her sides were an occupational hazard of long days at her desk. And a reminder that she should probably invest in an exercise bike in the New Year. Just as her slippered feet touched the floor, her phone chimed.

How do you feel about making Christmas ornaments instead? There's a place outside of Northampton that's not far.

"You've got to be kidding me." She couldn't seem to tear her eyes away from the screen.

"What? What did he say?" Beth scrambled up. "Don't tell me—"

"I'm not really sure what's going on here." Her heart shrank, even as the pressure in her chest expanded. Owen seemed too nice to get a kick out of teasing her for the book she wrote. And if he was, how did he figure out she'd written it?

"It's the ornaments, isn't it?" Beth's voice was edged with caution, and even though the room was too dim to make out her features, she knew her lips were probably pressed in a thin line, her brow creased.

A long breath escaped Grace's lips. She was really into Owen, and he just didn't seem like the type to mess with someone. "I think he might be following the book, but I don't think he knows I'm the author. He's too sweet."

"So what's your next move?" Beth stood and gathered the empty wine bottle and the barely touched meadow disks posing as cookies.

"Do the glassblowing, then take responsibility for the next date. After we hang out here and just relax, maybe he'll believe me that I really am okay not doing anything in particular." She'd practically given up on finding a nice, down-to-earth guy, and then Owen had stepped into the picture and gave her a glimpse of hope. What she was interested in was getting to know him, not where they were going or what they were doing. If the women in his life had told him he wasn't romantic, and then he started reading her book with its carousel of outings and never any downtime, she wouldn't blame him for swearing off dating altogether.

Chapter Eight

*"On the fourth date of Christmas, their gazes weren't
the only things smoldering. (When in a glassblowing
studio, bring proper hydration. It is very, very
hot...even before you look at your date.)"*
—The Twelve Dates of Christmas *by Paige Turner*

A T FIVE MINUTES to two, Owen spotted Grace behind
the wheel of a four-door sedan in fireball red pulling
into the parking lot. The color of her vehicle made him
smile. Of course her car, like her clothes and accessories,
would be lively and bold like her. The woman loved every
blinding shade on the color wheel. He turned off his igni-
tion, abruptly cutting off the heat streaming from the vents
and the music resonating through the speakers. Grace's head
was bent, looking at her phone, so he took his time getting
out of the car to walk over.

The slam of his driver's-side door reverberated through
the still afternoon air. The sun was peeking out through
leaden clouds that threatened to uphold the daily flurries the
area had been experiencing. Ice-covered snow cracked under
the soles of his shoes as he made his way to Grace's car. She
was getting out, a fuchsia scarf fringed with tassels wrapped
snugly around her neck. Her hair was swept up in a wavy

ponytail that swished as she walked toward him. She smiled, a bright flash of luminous teeth and glossy lips, and all of the oxygen whooshed from his lungs.

"Hey. Did you find the place okay?" Internally pinching himself for rubbing his hand over his hair, he dropped his arm stiffly to his side. At this rate the tumbleweed would ignite the moment he neared the kilns.

"Yeah. What a great idea." Her eyes were bright, and she looped her arm through his as they walked to the door. The door handle was ice against his bare skin as he held the door open. Grace walked in ahead of him, her fruity scent floating in her wake. He drew the fragrance into his lungs and stepped directly inside a gift shop. Poured concrete floors and exposed piping along the ceiling gave the place an industrial feel. The owners had played up the theme, hanging gears and cogs along the walls and metal shelving. The monochromatic color scheme showcased the merchandise. Blown glass pieces in all sizes, shapes, and colors looked like gemstones tossed on a frozen lake. Grace was walking around a table in the center of the room, eyes glued to an evergreen tree forged from iron. Each branch was a resting place for a glass ornament, twisting and catching the lights from above on translucent fishing lines.

"You guys my two o'clock private lesson?" A melodic voice cut through the still air like silver bells. He glanced up at a girl who could be no more than twenty. The tips of her blond hair were various shades of the rainbow, an apron was tied several times around her slight frame. She clunked forward on heavy work boots and offered a smile. "Oh, you are totally the cutest couple I've had so far this week."

"I, ah…think we might be. The two o'clock I mean. Not the cutest couple, that would be arrogant of me—" Heat prickled his cheeks, swarming over his back and neck.

The girl just laughed and swatted her hand in the air. "I got you. I'm Phoenix by the way, and I'll be helping you perfect your blowing skills."

"I don't have any skill. This is my first time." Hadn't he signed up for the introductory lesson?

Grace made a choking sound, then coughed a few times, face muffled against the inside of her elbow. Oh geez. He didn't mean… Another wave of heat blazed up his cheeks, and he was momentarily speechless. Grace rallied for him, introducing them both, and telling Phoenix to lead the way. They started down a long hall. Every few feet there was a glass star or heart. Once his face didn't feel like a raging inferno, he leaned over and whispered into Grace's ear.

"I'm going to call you Gutter-head Grace from this point forth." His tone must have been louder than he anticipated, because their instructor let out a single bark of laughter before slapping her hand over her mouth.

"Okay, Oblivious Owen." Grace did nothing to quiet her usual tone, and Phoenix's shoulders began silently shaking as she continued to walk ahead of them.

The hallway opened up to large workspace, and the temperature went from glacial to sauna the farther they walked into the room. Steel worktables and tools that looked like medieval torture devices were stored around the room. He silently cursed Paige Turner for false advertising. This was not romantic.

"Okay, so this is the part of the lesson where everyone

needs to listen up. One. Treat the tools and surfaces in the hot shop like you would molten lava, because essentially that's what we're working with. Two. Don't get distracted. Three. Drink water often. Four. Keep your safety goggles on at all times." She continued on, checking off the items on her fingers. "Five. Never hold the blowpipe higher than your head, and six, be aware of where your partner is in the room before making any turns or movements."

An uneasy tangle snowballed in his gut, as visions of third-degree burns danced in his head. "We can go if you want," he whispered to Grace. *Please want to go.*

"No way." She shushed him and focused her gaze on their instructor.

"This is our blowpipe." Phoenix gestured toward a long metal instrument. "We're going to use this to retrieve molten glass from the furnace."

"Oh, lovely," he muttered under his breath. Grace gave his arm a light swat and smiled at him. They both watched as Phoenix dipped the blowpipe into the furnace, gently rotated the tool, then stepped back. At the tip of the pipe was a glob of smelted glass that looked like gooey taffy…except it was the candy of nightmares, not dreams.

"That's so cool." Grace clapped her hands together once and watched with an eager expression.

"We're going to dip our glass into crushed granules." Phoenix walked with quick strides across the room to a bowl filled with shards of room-temperature glass and coated the terrifying taffy. "Then we take it over to this beauty." She gestured to what appeared to be a scaled version of the Eye of Sauron from *The Lord of The Rings.* He used his sleeve to wipe away the beads of sweat forming on his forehead. It certainly felt like he was in the bowels of Mordor. "We call this the glory hole," Phoenix said with pride. "This furnace polishes and softens the glass."

"How hot is it?" He raised a brow toward the feral piece of equipment, glowing a menacing yellow and orange.

"About two thousand degrees," Phoenix said cheerfully.

Sweet, merciful—

"No wonder it's so nice and steamy in here." Grace watched Phoenix with wide eyes, occasionally bouncing on the tips of her toes to get a better look.

They took turns creating their own glass ornaments under the instructor's supervision. He was hesitant with the tools, but Grace caught on right away, warming the glass, and dipping it in the crushed granules several times. She was a natural. Her ponytail curled into spirals in the hot atmosphere, and there was a rosy glow over Grace's face. She looked happy and satisfied as she carried out the steps. His chest expanded as he followed her movements.

"Whoa," Phoenix called out, breaking his train of thought. "Keep that hunk of burnin' love upright, Owen." She started to pace across the room toward him, arms already stretching forward.

He glanced down at the tool he was holding. The blow-pipe bobbed perilously in his hands before he could steady it, almost bumping his glass against the floor. *Mortifying.* The instructor stopped six feet in front of him, and released a drawn-out breath with her hand over her heart.

"Grace, what is the second most important rule for the hot shop?" Phoenix called out like a battle-hardened drill sergeant.

"Don't get distracted," Grace echoed back with the same militant pitch.

"Yes! No matter how pretty your partner is, keep your eyes on the glass." Phoenix smiled to herself, looking pleased by their exchange.

Was that really necessary? Phoenix seemed to be getting a kick out of his torment.

As the class went on, they used a steel table to roll and cool the glass for shaping. He was trying to be more aware of what he was doing, but it was hard not to notice the curls forming at the nape of Grace's neck, or the strand that had loosened near her forehead. Her flushed, dewy skin did funny things to the rhythm of his heart. Or maybe it was the intense heat.

"Now, come rest your pipes on this stand," Phoenix called. "Owen, how about you first."

Owen walked over to their instructor and propped the blowpipe in the divot of the stand.

"Okay, that's perfect. Now breathe into the pipe. See how you're creating the bubble?" He actually was doing it. His ball of lava was turning into something more interesting. How was he actually enjoying this? He'd never been a creative person. Sure, he appreciated art and music, but he hadn't thought it would be something he'd like actually learning. Never straying far from his typical activities—computers, tech stuff, gaming—had seemed natural, but maybe broadening his scope of hobbies was a good thing. Maybe he'd chosen a safe set of activities he could excel at. That didn't help him grow as a person though, or understand other people's perspectives.

They continued to work side by side, heating the glass before manipulating it with tweezers to learn different shapes and textures that could be achieved.

Phoenix finished off the last parts of the project for them, coating their work in additional clear glass from the furnace. She explained that was how the ornament appeared to have the colors encased inside, and helped them make a hole for a string if they wanted to hang it up. The instructor helped Grace roll the glass into a ball with a wet, wooden tool, before removing the creation from the pipe and into the fire-resistant gloves of another instructor.

"That was an amazing experience." Grace beamed at him as she watched the instructors walk their pieces back to the kiln where they'd slowly cool over twenty-four hours.

"I wasn't expecting to like that as much as I did. I mean, the time with you yes, but the actual creating? It kind of threw me at first." He handed her another bottle of water from the nearby cooler and sat next to her on the bench.

"Why did you bring me then?" Grace tilted her head, and her hair draped to the side.

"It was an idea I thought you might like." She searched his face for one heartbeat, then two until he shifted his stance beneath her gaze.

"I don't know about you, but I could use some cold air after being tucked in here. Why don't we go for a walk through town?" She placed the water bottle on the bench beside her and stood, hands instantly going to the apron strings at her back. "Why did I double knot this thing?" she grumbled, twisting ninety degrees as she struggled.

He chuckled and pushed to his feet. "You know, I think you actually just tied another knot."

"I'm glad you find this amusing," she said with a smile. In a hasty move, she slipped the loop over her neck and tried to shimmy the apron over her hips. Even in a struggle to untie herself, she moved like water, fluid.

"Let me." He didn't recognize the smoky grit invading his vocal cords as he placed a hand on either shoulder, gently turning her. The long-sleeve cotton shirt she wore was thin, and his fingers instantly registered the intimate strength in her shoulders, the delicate curve of her back. Her tart cherry scent peppered the air, making his mouth water. He moved trembling hands to her lower back and began working at the knot. Her shirt had ridden up in the struggle, making it impossible not to touch her bare skin as he untangled the strings. "Almost there." His voice had dropped another octave, truck tires over gravel. Maybe he just shouldn't talk, because there was no way Grace was missing the implications of his hoarse tone. When the thread finally gave way, she looked over her shoulder at him, lips open and inviting. He swallowed. Hard.

"I'll go hang this up." He took the apron from her hands. His legs ate up the floor as he put distance between them, needing that separation to slow his frantic heart. Liking the lesson wasn't the only thing that threw him today. The depth of his reactions to Grace was like a direct hit to the solar plexus. He hated to admit it, but maybe those first couple dates had been a result of his desire to prove to all the women he'd dated before that he could be spontaneous and romantic. That they'd let a good thing go. And maybe he'd chosen Grace because she was out of his league. He was the plain, nondescript T-shirt folded beside the tie-dyed, bedazzled one that was Grace. He wasn't sure how they ended up in the same drawer, but one thing was certain.

Their differences had done nothing, absolutely nothing, to stop him from falling for her.

WHEN OWEN AND Grace exited the glass studio at nearly five o'clock, a dusky veil blanketed the sky. Lights were sprinkled everywhere, like an upturned jar of glitter had dusted the town. The cozy warmth of Owen's gloved hand contented her as they walked through the winter wonderland. The spark that had rambled over her skin as Owen untied her apron was still fresh in her mind, and she'd needed the open air to unwind. The glassblowing was an awesome experience, but it was watching Owen's reaction that had been the most enjoyable part of the day. When he first saw what they'd be doing in the hot shop, he'd been totally out of his element. The equipment was clumsy in his hands, and he moved around like everything was liable to spontaneously combust. Then he'd gotten lost in it. The moment he started making the bubble in the glass, realized that he was creating something beautiful, his hesitation dissolved.

His movements were lighter and more confident. There was a sort of wonder and pride reflected in his eyes when he looked at his completed creation. He'd achieved so much: slews of awards for building designs that could hold up to disasters, were sustainable and green, (yes, detective Beth printed out a thirty-page document of press releases, industry articles, even his resume—*the creep*) and yet he'd been in awe of a brilliantly molded piece of glass that could fit between two hands. All while he'd designed skyscrapers, bridges, and even hospitals.

Owen squeezed her hand, bringing her back to the present. Streetlamps cast a sheen over snow-lined sidewalks, and residential lights added pops of color every few feet. They came upon a square in the center of the small town with a gazebo bathed in tiny lights that swirled up the spindles to the double roof and cupola. The structure sheltered a big balsam fir, and the image looked like it was snipped from a magazine. She was lost in the picture-perfect scenery when something solid smacked against her back. Spinning around, she found Owen already packing a tight ball of snow.

She grinned and dove into action. His shy side was slipping away, revealing all of the fun, playful angles of his personality.

"And here I was under the impression you played fair." Grace gave the snowball a final squeeze and sent it soaring through the air. And missed.

"Guess I didn't have to be concerned about my odds." He chuckled and raced around the side of the gazebo.

"So I'm a little rusty. Winter only comes once a year." Two clumps of snow flew at her in quick succession, and she dodged left, then right before crouching down. Grace scooped up the snow, forming one ball after another. It hadn't escaped her that Owen was doubling back around, trying to sneak up behind her. She'd be ready for him though. Whirling when his footfalls grew closer, she pelted him with everything in her arsenal, barely looking to see if she hit her mark before throwing again. When she glanced up, wet snow was sliding down his fogged-up glasses, clinging to his hair, and peppering his jacket.

"I guess I spoke too soon," he laughed, ruffling the top of her head.

When was the last time she'd had that much spontaneous fun? "You know, Santa was probably watching when you threw the first snowball." She raised a brow, enjoying the way his hair spiked up in disarray. Hair she'd love to run her fingers through.

"What are you saying?" A dimple indented the left side of his cheek. So. Freaking. Cute.

"I'm saying that coal isn't out of the question, mister." She stood up, brushing off her wet jeans and jacket.

"Better under my tree than in the air. Besides, as long as someone I really like doesn't mind being associated with someone on the Naughty List, I'm at peace with my decision." He raked his hands through his hair, sending pieces of snow flying to the ground.

"You know, it might be a good idea for someone on the Naughty List to spend even more time with someone on the Nice List." She tucked her hand into his, and they swung their arms in a blithe motion as they headed in the direction of their cars.

Light twinkled in his eyes. "It'll have to be immediate. It's a pretty dire situation."

"Tomorrow?" She angled her chin to meet his eyes.

"Let me plan something fun, and I'll text you later tonight." He gave her hand a double squeeze as she tried to recall the fifth outing of *The Twelve Dates of Christmas*.

"Nothing fun," she blurted out too fast.

Owen scrunched up his face. "What?"

"Let's just hang out." She internally sighed as Owen surveyed her with a wary expression. "I'm not someone who says they want to stay in, then gets upset when it actually happens."

The parking lot where they'd left the cars was just a few feet away now, and Owen paused on the sidewalk and turned toward her. "Yeah. It's just…"

"What?" Her pulse bounded beneath her skin, as she waited for him to speak. Maybe he was going to tell her about the book he was reading. Her book. She caught her bottom lip between her teeth.

"I found this list of holiday dates. I thought it would be fun to do them together." He gently twisted a loose curl at her shoulder around his finger before releasing it.

Grace swallowed hard. *Oh man.* Was he referring to the list in her romance novel? The one the hero made to impress the heroine and save her from lackluster dating? For the first time, she wished the book hadn't survived the publication process. If Owen was referring to her book, and found out she'd written it, he'd put even more pressure on himself to execute those flawless dates. Present-day Grace wasn't concerned with that stuff, and she had a feeling Owen would prefer some quality downtime to decompress and get to know each other. She wanted that too. To know the real Owen. To see him in his own space, where he was most comfortable.

She gave a brisk shake of her head. "How many activities were on this list?"

"About twelve," he said, chipping at the snowbank with the side of his foot.

Good grief. What were the odds? "Maybe we can deviate from the list. If you really prefer to get out, how about I plan something?"

"I don't know." A shy smile played over his lips. "Will it involve activities frowned upon by the surgeon general?"

Only Owen. She schooled her expression like she did when Beth's mom asked about the amount of wine consumed in their apartment. "I promise I'll return you with all limbs intact, squeaky-clean lungs, and a seminutritious meal in your stomach." They closed the distance to the parking lot, and Owen walked her to her car. His hand on the small of her back sent a shiver of pleasure coursing down her back.

"Okay, then. Night, Grace." He reluctantly let go of her hand, so she could get into her car. She was much happier to have her fingers laced with Owen's opposed to curled around the cold steering wheel.

"Night, Owen." She gave a little wave, and wondered if someone had created a Fitbit that recorded smiles throughout the day. A small part of her was apprehensive that the reason she'd connected with Owen so thoroughly, so quickly was because he'd mirrored the ideas of her hero—someone she was intimately connected with because she'd created him. Did her brain and her heart both recognize that Owen had showed Grace a secret glimpse of those old inner fantasies, and in response thought, *This is the one!* Or was it simply Owen himself warming her thoughts and tangling her up inside?

Chapter Nine

"And on the fifth date of Christmas, his feelings piled up high, just like the snow falling in thick sheets outside. Beautiful and terrifying all at the same time. (Hint: Christmas Eve engagement = annual anniversary reminder.)"
—The Twelve Dates of Christmas *by Paige Turner*

OWEN AND GRACE were flying. That was the only word suitable for the rate of speed at which their inflated tube rocketed down the steep hill of glazed snow. The evergreens lining the slope blurred past, a green curtain ruffling on either side of the mountain. Wind rang in Owen's ears and slipped down the neck of his winter jacket. Grace let out a cheer as they hit a bump, the momentum lifting them up, up. He stiffened, Isaac Newton's iconic quote on the brain, and prepared for the hard whack when the tube hit the ground. As expected, nature's slide slammed into his backside, and he held on to Grace, who was sitting between his legs. She raised her hands above her head like one might on a roller coaster, a machine that was equipped to defy the physical properties of gravity. The inertia from the sled wouldn't be stopped by an engineer's wheel design.

"This thing should have seat belts," Owen called over the

air whipping around them.

Her laugh rang out, and he was sure if he saw her face, there'd be a huge smile stretching over her lips. This was a new experience for him. His parents were wonderful, but he and his sister had a sheltered upbringing. Any activity they engaged in had called for multiple layers of protective gear. He was positive they'd never made mud pies. Bouncy castles and trampolines had been strictly off-limits. Sage did a mad sweep of her house every time their parents stopped by for a visit, putting all teeth-rotting sweets into a secret container. She always missed one or two things and got the dreaded disapproving eye.

As the slope evened out, their tube slowed, and Grace planted her heels into the snow like brakes.

"If we go too far, we'll have to walk all the way back to the rope tow." Grace put her hands on her snowsuit-clad knees and stood up, turning to offer her hand to him. The pulley system was in varying stages of use with riders attaching their tubes at the bottom for a lift all the way back to the top, while others had reached the peak and were buzzing down the hill. An attendant helped hook their tube to a safety latch, and they jumped back in to relax on the ride up.

"What'd you think?" They were both sitting with their legs crossed, facing each other. Their knees overlapped in the small space, and every shift or bump made the hairs on the back of his neck stand up with renewed awareness of their proximity. He was still hanging on to the handles, gloves covering his knuckles, which were probably blanched with effort. Grace looked like she was sitting on a cozy couch, leaning back with her elbows propped behind her on the edge of the tube.

"Fast. It was fast." His heart lifted when Grace beamed back at him. Being with her gave him a special kind of lightness, similar to the coming of Christmas as a child.

"I think you liked it. You just don't want to admit it." She purposely bumped his knee with hers, and a shock jolted up his thigh and gathered between his hips. "What was your favorite part?"

He'd liked holding her close on the way down the hill. The feel of her body tucked neatly against his. The scent of her hair mingling with fresh pine and the brisk slap of wind. He liked the way the cold air kissed her skin, leaving rosy imprints on the apples of her cheeks and nose. He liked the sound of her laughter, free and wild, rising overhead as they whipped down the slope. "I liked a lot of things," he said, eyes locked on hers. His voice had permanently adopted a gruff tone around Grace, his attraction audible in each syllable. Her eyes widened, darkened as if she'd heard every secret thought that had just played through his mind.

He cleared his throat, trying to regain some of the dignity his voice gave away. "The rope system was a great idea, especially for families with young kids." It was better to move the subject off him, off them, with so many feelings swirling. Feelings that went beyond like, and rolled into uncharted territory in a covered wagon. Hopefully this ended better than his early games of *The Oregon Trail. You have died of dysentery. The wagon has tipped, you lost two-hundred pounds of food.* Maybe fording the river in a pixelated wagon during computer class had suppressed his courage to take risks. He wasn't good with new and preferred to stick to routine, but Grace was showing him that different could be exciting. "But I think it takes away the physical activity part of the sport."

"And that, my friend, is the very best part. Not everyone is a beacon of impeccable fitness." They laughed as the tube inched up the slope. The view was something else. The roll of powdered snow, the rise and fall of the mountain range in the distance, and the glow of light at the center of the horizon, a soft, hazy blue with a gold filter.

When they got to the top of the hill, they got off the tube, and he dragged it closer to the middle of the slope.

"Let's go down sitting like we were on the rope tow." Enthusiasm coated Grace's words as she got into the tube with her legs facing the center of the sled, back up against the inflated lip.

"Are you sure?" He climbed into the tube, back into the same position they'd sat in minutes ago.

"Beth and I have gone down this way before. It's like a twister."

Oh joy.

"Here, cross your arms like this," she said, making an X from her forearms. "And hold my hands." He mirrored her position, gripping her hands. *Oh, yes, this was perfectly safe now.*

"One problem, how do we push off?" he asked, gauging the distance of the slope and trying to determine the potential rate of speed.

"Just move around like this, and we'll inch closer to the edge."

He didn't want to think of Grace wiggling her hips right

now. Something that would stir up all kinds of trouble in this sitting position. So, he rocked the tube with her, and they slowly slid toward the edge.

"Okay, you ready for this?" Grace shouted when they'd reached the point of no return.

He had to be careful not to squeeze her hands to the point of crushing them once they got going.

"Engage!" he called out, surprising himself. Grace's way of looking at the world, of experiencing everything was infectious. One second they were teetering on the top of the slope and the next they were whirling down like a spinning top. Grace leaned in closer and gripped his hands tightly, keeping her body low against the succession of pirouettes. He leaned in closer to Grace and realized she was giggling. He caught her eye as they continued their descent, and a laugh bubbled from his own lips. His sides were aching by the time the tube slowed to a whir of a carousel ride. Grace was gasping for air as they slipped past the stop for the rope tow.

"No," Grace said with all the air left in her lungs. A deep chuckle burst from his lips as she leaned over the edge of the tube, holding her arms in the direction of the rope tow, groaning as their free ride slipped farther away.

She took a shallow breath and laughed, "I don't want to walk back." That did it. They were both still rolling with laughter long after the tube had stopped much, much farther down the hill. Tears were flowing from Grace's eyes, and he was puffing out quick bursts of breath fighting for control over the rolls of laughter. When they'd finally calmed, he looked up, and Grace was staring at him. She lifted her hand

and placed it on his cheek. "That was fun," she murmured. His breath caught, loosening another type of control within him. She leaned in, dropping her eyes to his lips.

A blur of blue moved in the corner of his vision, and he quickly looked to his left. "Whoa," he yelled as the other tube careened down the hill, poised for a direct hit to Grace. He dug his hand into the snow and pushed out of the way, trying to lessen her impact by increasing his. The other tube slammed into his arm. The one that was currently anchored in the snow. Pain shot up his wrist to his elbow. He hadn't heard a cracking sound, more of an unsettling sort of pop. Grace was up and out of the tube, laying into the three teenagers who had, in their defense, stopped to apologize.

"Oh my gosh. Are you okay? Can you lift your arm?" She rushed back to the tube and knelt in the snow beside him.

"I'm fine," he assured her and used both arms to try to stand. The slight pressure on his arm felt like a metal skewer running up his wrist. He groaned, and Grace's eyes went wide with panic.

"I am so, so sorry. I'll carry you back to the car." Her arms were wrapped around his waist and tugged him into a standing position.

"Please don't try to lift me. My legs aren't hurt. I can walk to the car." He tried to keep his left arm still as they started to walk. Grace stood on his right side and kept a firm grip on his good arm.

"And then the car is taking you straight to the hospital." Her voice was insistent. She bit her lip and kept her eyes fixed on him, like he was going to drop at any moment as they walked toward the parking lot.

"Really, it's okay. It's a little sore. I think it just needs some ice, not a doctor." The withering glance she gave him was enough to stop his protests about a trip to the hospital, but he still wanted to see what it looked like first. By the time they got to the car, a sharp ache was buzzing around his elbow joint and wrist.

"Let's take off your coat and see if there's any swelling." Grace's hands were on the cuff of his jacket, gently inching the material in a downward motion so it slipped off of his shoulder. The next part was going to be trickier. He could already tell the fabric of the other sleeve was bound tight against his arm. The swelling had started the moment the other tube rammed them. He just hadn't wanted to concern Grace any more than she already was. And yes, he was trying to act tough when he wanted to whimper like a baby.

Grace walked behind him, sweeping her fingers beneath the collar of the jacket as she began to ease it over his left shoulder. Once the fabric got to his elbow though, it was stuck.

Her breath was quick and shallow as her gaze looked over the swollen limb, visible even below the fabric of his coat that refused to budge. "Why did you act like this was nothing all the way to the car?"

"It's not so bad." *It was so bad.* Yellow spots started to pop up in the corners of his eyes. Probably not a good sign.

"Your arm is the size of a Brawny paper towel roll," she hissed, still carefully trying to manipulate the fabric over his too-large arm. "We're going to have to cut this." She looked at the sleeve with disdain.

"They'll have scissors at the emergency room," he said, as his focus wavered. Grace was right, he couldn't ignore this. Why did he have to experience his first sprain or broken arm on a date with Grace? "I think I need to sit down."

"Right, sorry." She ran around him and opened the passenger-side door. He eased in, trying not to jar his arm further. "And don't worry. I have scissors in my purse."

"Who carries scissors in their purse?" he muttered to himself as she slammed the door and sprinted to the driver's side.

"Thank goodness I wrapped Aunt May's birthday present on-the-go the other day." She fished through her bag, receipts, candy wrappers, a pair of socks flying into the center console. Her purse was an organizational nightmare.

"What do you mean by wrapping on-the-go?" He leaned against the headrest and closed his eyes. Colors bounced behind his lids, and sweat was beading down his back beneath his knit sweater.

"Exactly like it sounds." She continued to rummage, unearthing a T-shirt, a flashlight, and a bruised apple.

"Good grief, woman. Did you go camping recently?" He would've been in stitches at the items coming out of her bag if he didn't hurt so much.

"Ah-ha." She drew out a pair of full-size kitchen scissors and held them up to the light. The steel glinted in the sun, making her look a little bit like Jack Nicholson from *The Shining.*

"Were you going to shear a sheep after wrapping the present? Cut a grand opening ribbon?" He moved back slightly, lifting a brow. His stomach was hard and churning from the pain, while Grace was looking a bit hysterical.

"Nope, just cutting the wrapping paper at red lights."

"Red lights aren't for gift wrapping! Especially with Stephen King scissors! Can you imagine the traffic violations? Oh hello, officer. Just boxing up a nice little gift while operating a three-thousand pound vehicle. Would you mind holding my tape for a moment? Oh, and was there a reason you're stopping me today?"

"Not everyone has the leisure of gift wrapping at home," she said, slipping the open mouth scissors in the tight place between his skin and coat. "Some. Of. Us. Are. Busy," she ground out as she used all her strength to wield the shears of Thor.

"Some of us are responsible stewards of road safety." A pounding ache started behind his eyes, matching the one pulsating at the core of his wounded arm. It worsened once the last stitch of his jacket frayed and Grace slid off the barrier containing his swollen limb.

"That. Is. Brutal." She whistled as she looked down at his arm, still growing in size. "Hang on. I'm going to get you to the hospital in record time."

"That's kind of what I'm afraid of," he groaned, and wondered if he'd survive Grace's distracted driving to get there.

Chapter Ten

"Romance is just what the doctor ordered.
(Well, mostly.)"
—The Twelve Dates of Christmas *by Paige Turner*

G RACE WAS SCUFFING up the linoleum floors of the ER waiting room. She'd been pacing for an hour, or at least that's what it felt like. How could he have played off his injury like it was no big deal? Like the space between his elbow and wrist hadn't doubled in size? She'd panicked when she'd seen the extent of the swelling. Not her proudest moment. Gosh, Owen must think her a witch for snapping at him when he was the injured party. She was just so worried. Owen's injury might not be life-threatening, but he relied on his arms to make a living. He probably had to draw blueprints, measure, calculate, and type. All difficult feats with a broken arm. Broken because he'd moved her side of the tube out of the way of the kids coming down the hill. He'd taken the impact so she wouldn't get hurt.

In a few short weeks, she'd learned a lot about Owen. Heck, he'd probably learned a lot about himself, too, between stepping outside his comfort zone with the glassblowing and saving her sorry hide for the second time. He pretended he wasn't brave, but he'd put himself in harm's way for her twice. Neither of those things had been a fluke like he wanted her to believe.

Clogs whacking against the tile floor startled her, and she glanced up in the direction of the noise.

A man in blue scrubs, with a tag that read RN, approached her. "Hi, I'm Brian. We talked earlier. Your friend asked if I could share a status update with you, and to let you know he can call a cab to take you home. The doctor just reviewed the X-ray results, and he doesn't have a fracture, but he has a severe sprain which will take anywhere from several weeks to months before he has his complete range of motion back without discomfort. We're fitting him with a splint to compress the injury and then we'll get his discharge paperwork ready."

"Please tell him I don't need a cab. I'm waiting." Did Owen think she'd really abandon him at the emergency room?

"It might be a while. We're a little backed up at the moment, but once he has all his paperwork, he'll be free to go." He moved to the side, giving a wider berth to a patient being pushed in a wheelchair.

"Thanks. I'll be right out here." She gestured to the waiting room, and the nurse nodded before disappearing through the doors for hospital staff only.

For the next hour, she read a book on her cell phone to pass the time. She wasn't sure what caught her attention, but suddenly she was sure Owen was in the room with her. She looked up, and he was coming out of the double doors that led to the patient rooms, injured arm secured in a removable splint and sling.

"Hey," she said, stuffing the phone in her bag and jumping to her feet. "How are you feeling?"

"A little woozy. They gave me some pain medicine, but I don't think I have a good tolerance for it." He wavered a bit, looking disoriented. Definitely someone who wouldn't have been allowed to drive home on his own. She was glad she'd waited, not that it was ever a question. If she hadn't, Owen would've needed to stay at the hospital even longer to wait for a ride.

"Okay," she said. "Time to get you out of here." Grasping his uninjured arm firmly, she led him through the crowded emergency room to the exit. "Want me to pull your car around?" The automatic glass doors slid open when they approached, frigid air embracing them with a quick smack as they stepped out onto the sidewalk.

"No, it's no problem. I can walk." He shook his head, shuffling his feet a bit as he moved, like even he was unsure of his footing.

She'd let him walk, because it was only a few steps from the front door. That and his ego would be bruised because he'd gotten hurt on a date with her. Something she felt terrible about. Hadn't she promised to return him in one piece? She helped him into the passenger's side of the car and rounded the hood to hop behind the wheel. She rubbed her hands together before gripping the ice block posing as a steering wheel. Grace started the car, turning on both the seat warmers and cranking the heat up to high.

Then she turned to Owen, who was staring at her with a loopy grin. The poor thing was so hopped up on pain meds. "I never had a chance to thank you. But I appreciate how you moved my part of the tube out of the way this afternoon. I'm so sorry it happened."

"Don't be. It wasn't your fault."

She held her hands up briefly to the vents where warm air was already circulating. "Still, I did promise to return you fully intact."

"And you did. You made no guarantee about other bodily harm, so I participated at my own risk." He struggled to draw the seat belt over his chest, so she took it from his right hand and snapped it in place.

"Okay, now that we're all strapped in, give me your address, and then try to rest a little." A tenderness unfurled in her chest as she looked across the car at Owen and the large sling keeping his arm plastered close to his body. He'd sacrificed his arm for her and had been so brave throughout the ordeal. The pull to look after him, at least until the medicine wore off, stacked inside her.

"Four Sleigh Maker Lane." His lids were starting to droop, but he shook his head, as if trying to shed exhaustion.

"That sounds pretty," she said, glancing at the backup camera and to her left and right before reversing out of the parking space. "I also wanted to say I'm sorry for being snippy when I discovered how hurt your arm was. It's a personality flaw. When someone I care about is hurt or upset, I get bossy and short-tempered, but it's just my way of trying to get control of the situation. It's something I'm working on."

A slow smile spread over his face, practically glowing with pleasure. "You said you care about me. You can't take it back now."

"Wasn't planning to," she chuckled, and eased around a curve in the road that glinted with ice.

"I care about you too, Grace."

Warmth from his words alone seeped through her skin, like hot cocoa and a cozy blanket on a chilly day. She'd only known Owen a short time, but her statement was the truth, she did care for him. Maybe a little too deeply. And that was what scared her. As much as she loved her single, carefree lifestyle, she could picture Owen in her future and see how he fit. The more time she spent with him, the more she was certain she wanted to embrace their relationship, introduce him to her parents and Nora (something she'd never done with a man before), and invite him to spend time with Beth.

She followed the instructions of the GPS, going past the center of town where the shops were glowing from the inside out, giving everything a homey, cheerful essence. The clusters of homes thinned as she drove on, streetlamps lighting the path to residential drives. She turned her directional on and pulled down Owen's street. His breathing had deepened with each mile; he was fast asleep. At the end of the private street, she found Owen's address, a large colonial-style home nestled on the edge of a cul-de-sac. Lights swirled over the landscaping and a scarlet bow was fixed to the light post. The moment she entered the drive, more lights sprang on, illuminating the front and side entrances. She chuckled internally as she thought of Owen's pursuit of efficient lighting. She parked the car in the driveway, unsure of how to open the garage door, and tapped Owen's outer thigh, not wanting to disturb his hurt arm.

"We're here," she said softly, and he stirred, eyes flickering opening.

"I can't believe I fell asleep knowing the size of the scissors you keep in your purse," he muttered, sleep hanging on to the threads of his voice.

"Your arm might still be locked inside your jacket without those scissors." Her muffled laugh filled the open space between them, and he smiled back.

"I'll come around." She unbuckled her seat belt and opened the door, treading carefully even though the driveway was plowed.

"I'm okay now," he said when she opened his door. "You don't have to worry."

Despite his statement, she still took his arm as they walked up the path to his front door.

"Your lights look beautiful."

"My nieces love driving through neighborhoods to look at Christmas lights. They'd lecture me if I didn't have them." His lips quirked, expression softened as he spoke of them.

Key in the lock, Owen opened the door, lights automatically flicking on. He gestured for her to go inside first and shut the door behind them. She'd call Beth for a late-night pickup once she was sure Owen was going to be okay on his own, but for now she stared in awe at the Christmas tree in the open living space. Its boughs were drooping with the weight of too many ornaments, pine needles smothered in gold tinsel, and a star hovered up top. "Your nieces decorate your tree, don't they?" She smiled, melting toward him even more.

"Sure do," he laughed. "Puts the tree to the test each year."

Her stomach chose that moment to growl, amplified by the empty house. Her cheeks heated, and she made a mental note to have Beth hit a drive-thru on the way back to the apartment.

"You know what? I'm hungry too. I'll make us something quick, and then we can call you a cab."

"Beth can come get me, and you're not doing anything in the kitchen. Why don't you find us something to watch on the television, and I'll go dig through your cabinets?"

"Make yourself at home," he chuckled. Once she was satisfied that Owen was sitting and not going to collapse in a heap on the floor, she went to check out the kitchen situation. Every feature in the kitchen made her swoon. Too bad she couldn't put it to good use. She was a terrible cook, and it wasn't like the cream and gold speckled granite countertops and island, the tile backsplash, or the glass-faced cupboards had anything to do with making actual food.

After a brief search, she found the makings for peanut butter and jelly sandwiches.

"Grace's gourmet PB&J," she announced as she entered the living room. "And potato chips. I know I promised a nutritious meal, but that was before the whole arm sprain thing."

"Sounds perfect. Thanks for making it." He took the plate she offered with a smile, and she sat beside him, crossing her socked feet beneath her.

"So, I guess the adventurous dates are off the table for the time being," he said after taking a bite and setting down his sandwich.

"Between the runaway horse sleigh and the tubing collision, I think we're better off staying inside." She crunched into a chip, salty and crisp, and reached for one of the glasses of water she'd poured.

"I'll have to take a look at that list and do some eliminating. Wreath making is probably out. Caroling was never on the table." He flicked his gaze to her, a crooked smile on his lips, one adorable dimple appearing on his side profile.

Laughter tumbled from her lips. "Oh, well…we don't need to follow the list. But no caroling, huh? Parading down Main Street, clutching tapered candles, spreading joy."

He gave her an uneasy look, leaning slightly away. "That's a hard pass."

A belly laugh shook her, and she gave him a playful nudge. "Really? Why? It's fun. Our parents and grandparents would take us every year, and it was always so magical, with the streetlights gleaming and the snow falling. We'd end with hot cocoa and warm candied pecans from the sweet shop at the end of the street."

"You probably enjoy it because you have a nice singing voice. Me? Not so much." He ate a lone piece of crust on his plate and slid it onto the coffee table.

"I really don't. Beth always complains about my shrill, nasally voice ringing in her ears for days afterward." She didn't take offense to Beth's teasing. It was just something they did, more like sisters than friends.

"If she only heard my voice. The only place that's appropriate for a voice like mine is a haunted house at Halloween. Maybe." He shook his head and angled his body toward her. "That one is a definite no for me."

She put her clear plate on the coffee table alongside his

and leaned back. "Okay then, we could always spend time here or at my place. Or I could chauffeur you around town looking at holiday lights."

"Much better. In fact, as long as there's no singing involved, heights, wheels or skis on my feet, I'll most likely try it." He started to remove the sling around his neck, hissed, and visibly paled.

"What are you trying to do?" She moved to the edge of the seat to give him more space.

"The doctor said to take off the splint and ice it every few hours." He gritted his teeth and removed the sling, just the splint left on his wounded arm. "I'm just going to grab ice."

"Owen." She placed a hand on his shoulder and stood. "Just stay there. I'll get it." Before he could protest, she took off toward the kitchen and found a plastic bag she'd seen in one of the drawers while making their sandwiches. The automatic icemaker made filling the bag easy work, then she took a dish towel and wrapped the bag so it wouldn't be too cold on Owen's skin. He'd been through enough today without adding frostbite to the mix.

"Here we go," she said, walking back into the living room. Crouching down, she placed the ice to the side and started to undo the Velcro of the splint.

"Thanks. You're much gentler than I am," Owen murmured. Had it suddenly dawned on him how very much alone they were in his house? Just the two of them?

Her heart sped up, breath hitched as she tried to focus on what she was doing beneath Owen's intense stare. She reached the last Velcro strap, but it had taken effort to keep her hands steady.

"Okay. Ready? I'm going to pull it off now." She waited for him to nod, and she carefully slid the splint over his thumb and hand. His arm was so stretched that the skin was shiny, and an angry bruise covered the area of impact. Her stomach clenched, guilt riding through her system. She placed the ice down, even as she felt his fingers playing with the tips of her hair.

"Thank you," he whispered, too much emotion filtering through his voice for creating a simple ice pack.

"Of course. No problem." She moved back to the couch next to him. "You scared me today."

"I never want you to get hurt on my watch, Grace." His back was to the arm of the chair, one leg folded against the cushion and one planted on the floor so they were facing each other.

"This is the second time you've put yourself in harm's way for me. No one has ever done that before." She reached out and took his right hand, and instantly a sense of belonging stole over her. A sense of rightness.

"Then they weren't faced with the opportunity." His thumb caressed her skin in small circles, her weightless feeling in her chest expanding with every touch. "Because you're a treasure, Grace." He leaned in and pressed a kiss on her forehead. A kiss that did make her feel treasured. Her heart was beating in hard, steady pumps, while her legs had gone weak on her. It was a good thing she wasn't standing, because she would have toppled over right then and there. Owen might not be classically romantic like her dad was with her mom, but he made her feel special in every way that counted. Who cared about flowers and moonlight when you had kindness and concern? Owen was turning out to be one of the most important people in her world. He was the first person who made her want to be tied down. And if she was honest with herself, she'd already fallen too fast to make that decision.

Chapter Eleven

"What is it about the holidays that gives the most mundane, routine task an air of magic? Even washing dishes is especially delightful. (Said no one. Ever.)
—The Twelve Dates of Christmas *by Paige Turner*

OWEN HAD SPENT more time with Grace over the past couple weeks, and Christmas was right around the corner—less than a week away. Since the tubing accident, he'd gotten a glimpse of Grace's softer side. Even though he reassured her that his arm was okay, she popped over to his house several times in the days following his injury. The fridge and freezer were brimming with casseroles and takeout containers. Now that he'd convinced her the worst of it was behind him, they'd met up several times for dinner after work during the week. They'd even driven through town, trying to find the very best Christmas light displays, and had roasted marshmallows on his back deck to make s'mores beneath the stars. There wasn't a time he'd been happier or more content than when he was with Grace.

He found himself whistling tunes at his desk, tapping his fingers to an invisible beat inside his head, or grinning stupidly during formal meetings. Owen had even mixed up his rotation of gray and tan shirts, throwing in some bright blues and yellows just because they reminded him of her. And that's how it felt, like she'd added a splash of color to his world. He'd never been unhappy, but Grace was like an explosion of glitter confetti over his very average life. She brought the extra sparkle.

The more he got to know Grace, the more he was sure they had started something lasting, but did she feel the same way? As his feelings rose higher, so did the stakes, the tension and the what-ifs snowballing in his mind. Too late to turn back now. She'd told him she didn't want to see anyone else, but that didn't mean she was looking for serious. The conversation had been on the tip of his tongue as embers crackled around their roasted marshmallows. Fear had clamped down on his vocal cords though. And the dates. Grace repeatedly told him they didn't matter—sometimes even seemed frustrated by them—but his ex's words were a constant whisper in his ear. That he should've done more to keep the spark alive, should've been more of a romantic. Grace wasn't Sarah, but now that he'd started following that list in the book it was hard to stop. Maybe their relationship was so blissful because of the dates. Without them, she'd eventually realize how normal and boring he was.

She might come to her senses and leave. There were so many ways Grace could break his heart, but it was better to know what you were working with, right? A solid building needed a blueprint, just like a strong relationship needed a plan. Communication. Partnership. He was going to bring it up tonight when she came over for dinner. Maybe.

"Owen, McClary just called a private meeting in his office." Percy Little, his coworker with an extensive collection of *Star Wars* ties, tapped on the glass wall and poked his head through the door to his office.

"What about?" Owen rolled back his chair so he could open his desk drawer. The neatly stacked pads of lined paper waited for moments like this, alongside the pens organized by color. He picked up one of each, stood, and followed Percy down the hall to their mutual destination—the boss's office. Owen was tall at six feet two inches, but Percy had at least four inches on him with legs that ate up the floor as he walked. They entered Mr. McClary's office, an identical copy of the other boxy, glass-walled cubicles. His desk was cluttered with paperwork, framed family photos, and two Bonsai trees that he religiously pruned.

"The state put out a bid for a new tunnel and overpass design." The boss leaned back in his rolling chair, surveying his team. "City Hall is collecting immediate proposals so they can allocate the budget to this fiscal year, and start construction in the spring. We're going to need all hands on deck to turn this project around. I know it's Friday, but can anyone put in some extra hours tonight? The more the better."

"I'm available." Owen spoke up first, followed by his coworker's unenthused grunts of acceptance. He was so used to his life revolving around his career, he hadn't thought twice before answering. In some instances, like this one, there were times when work would have to come first, but he couldn't fall into the habit of volunteering when he and Grace had plans. The hours he put in had been a dealbreaker in his past relationships. His feelings for Grace were deeper than for anyone he'd dated before, and he was committed to putting the time and effort into their relationship. Grace had a demanding job of her own, and he was sure there were times she'd have to cancel because something came up at her job. She'd understand why he had to move their plans for tonight, so long as it didn't become a habit. He scrunched his brow. What had his ex said? *You're too busy with your career to put time into anything serious.* Grace was different though. With her, serious was much more appealing.

He'd never been able to picture sharing his space with another person, or imagine a future with one of the women he'd dated beyond the next month or two. When Owen got back to his desk after the impromptu meeting, he closed his eyes for a brief moment, trying to imagine what it would be like to be with Grace three months from now, a year, five. His heart slowed, and the world came swirling to a stop. He could picture her bright clothes hanging in the closet beside his, her toothbrush and cherry shampoo in the bathroom. Before Grace, he was content to spend quiet weekends decompressing. Would Grace find that lifestyle boring? Always seeking some form of excitement? His phone rang, and he glanced at the screen.

"Hi. I was just about to call you." An involuntary smile spread over his lips like it always did when he heard Grace's voice.

"Oh, everything all right?" He heard the click of a keyboard on the other line. It was nearly five o'clock, almost time for her to leave the office.

"Yeah, but something came up, a new project at work. Want to come over to my place tomorrow instead?" He'd expected to wait a bit, maybe be greeted with a long pause.

She did neither.

"That works for me. Beth will be thrilled. Her mom phoned to let her know she was flying in for a surprise visit." Her voice dipped into annoyed territory, papers shuffled, a stapler clicked.

"Is that a welcome surprise?" He laughed, because the stories he'd heard about the dynamic between Beth and her mother were amusing.

"Like finding your first gray hair. Beth just went out to buy cleaning supplies. She'll have a vacuum strapped to my back Ghostbuster-style the minute she arrives home." Metal keys clinking together chimed over the line, and he imagined her tossing the full ring haphazardly into the black hole that she referred to as a purse.

"Sorry about that." He cringed. Grace wasn't into cleaning, so wielding a vacuum or washing windows wasn't something he imagined to be high on her list of priorities.

"It's for the best. If I leave her to her own devices, she'll probably throw out half of my things. Anyway, good luck with the project. See you tomorrow."

"Night. Make sure you have good ventilation with all those cleaning supplies." They said their goodbyes, and he started to turn back to the project recap in his inbox. First though, there was something on his mind. He opened the desk drawer and took out *The Twelve Dates of Christmas*. There'd been one date that he'd wanted to do more than the rest, even though he changed it a bit to what Grace might like better, and that flexed his engineering skills.

Dates for Grace

1. ~~Hot cocoa at quaint café~~
2. ~~Horse-drawn sleigh—ask Grace to lunch after? Check Yelp.com restaurant ratings.~~
3. ~~European Christmas market~~
4. ~~Glassblowing ornaments—dangerous???~~
5. ~~Sledding~~
6. ~~Caroling~~ NOT A CHANCE
7. Baking and decorating cookies
8. ~~Looking at neighborhood lights—not sure if Grace would like this.~~
9. ~~Roast marshmallows over fire outside—messy??~~
10. ~~Pillow fort, eggnog, holiday music, fire—~~igloo + wine + stars?
11. Holiday movie marathon
12. Wreath-making class

He'd expected to get to the tenth date of Christmas before now, but with his arm injury it hadn't been possible. Grace was going to be mad at him for using his arm, but really it was fine. Plus, once they were cozied up in their igloo with the stars shining above, she'd probably wouldn't be too upset.

Engineering structures was one of the things he excelled at. Grace would be able to experience something he'd designed. What others thought about his personality or his work shouldn't matter, so long as he was doing his best, but he craved Grace's acceptance and approval although she readily gave both. At some point, he had to stop devaluing himself, build up his confidence, and own who he was as a person. Why had he ever thought little things like his hot cocoa preference would matter to Grace? Never mind what pretending to be more adventurous, exciting would've gotten him. He'd already wrangled a runaway horse sleigh, made a glass paperweight in a two-thousand degree furnace and nearly dropped it on his toes, and received a very sprained arm. He'd had enough adventure on his dates with Grace to last a lifetime.

What did it mean that he kept coming back for more?

Chapter Twelve

*"On the tenth date of Christmas, cozy spaces and sweet
embraces were not in short supply (swoon)."*
—The Twelve Dates of Christmas *by Paige Turner*

G RACE LIFTED HER hand and rapped on the front door
of Owen's house again. She was early—way early, but
she came bearing his favorite classic hot cocoa from the
coffee shop they visited on that first day. She leaned in,
pressing her ear to the frosty door and didn't hear the sound
of footsteps. His car was there, so he might be doing laundry
or taking a nap, which was not like Owen at all. The nap
part, not the laundry part. She shrugged and walked down
the steps toward the garage. Owen had given her the code to
open it, and there was a key beneath the mat for instances
like this, or if she got out of work early, but she still preferred
to knock first. Using the key, she let herself in.

The place was immaculate as usual, unlike her space,
which was in crisis mode. She'd forgotten what color the rug
was at this point. Her boots tapped against the floor as she
ambled into the kitchen to set down the container of gingerbread people she'd made. It had been fun decorating them
with silly frosting faces, iced smiles, and candy clothes,
knowing it would make Owen smile. He didn't expect

surprises, which made her all the more eager to spoil him. She moved into the living room. "Owen?" Huh. Maybe he really was napping. A flash of blue caught her eye and she spun toward the sliding glass doors that led to the backyard. She drew in a quick breath—what in the world was Owen doing outside? With his injured arm? He had a shovel in one hand and was standing in a hole waist-deep. She flipped the lock on the slider and stepped out onto the deck. The railing along the set of stairs was coated in ice and slid against her skin, but she barely registered the cold.

"What are you doing?" Snow hit midcalf as she struggled over to Owen. He waved, one gloved hand leaving the blocks of snow he'd been packing together.

"Hey, Grace." He gave her a sheepish smile. Darn those dimples. "You're early. I was hoping to finish this up—"

"So I wouldn't see you using your arm?" She placed her hands on her hips. Owen was constantly trying to do sweet things, but at what cost to him?

There he went with that hand-in-the-cookie-jar grin. "And because I wanted to surprise you. That list I was telling you about? It gave me the idea." With one hand braced on the snow, he leaped out of the hole. "I changed it though, to something that might suit us better."

Every time it seemed they'd escaped the list, Owen brought it back up. His heart was in the right place, but she didn't need to be entertained or impressed by outings and activities. He wowed her on his own. They had lively conversations that had a smile spreading over her lips long after he left. At some point, he'd gotten the wrong impression of her. She wasn't the woman from her book, but then again, there was no way for him to know she'd written it. Was she still projecting that image? Of a girl who needed to be swept away by a man? She'd never abandon her independence or identity. A partner, someone to share life's ups and downs with, and spend time with. Those were the things she valued at this point in her life.

"Now I'm here to help. You can take this hot cocoa, relax, and give me instructions. I don't want you hurting yourself to do something sweet for me."

"Grace…" A tuft of hair was poking out from beneath his hat, and his scarf was slightly askew. Tenderness welled up inside her. She loved how giving he was, but he should expect the same in return. He'd looked shocked when she'd come to check on him after his injury. Even more so at the soup and meals she'd made. A relationship required both parties to participate, not just one who did all the work. Yes, her dad might surprise her mom with pillow forts filled with roses or whisk her off to a swoon-worthy weekend destination, but her mother showed her father affection in other ways. She took care of him by keeping his favorite drinks stocked in the fridge, preparing his lunch—one that always had a note and a cartoon drawing. Would Owen ever allow their relationship to be a partnership too?

"You got me hot chocolate?" He crossed over to her and placed his hands along her arms. "Thank you." The appreciation reflecting in his eyes was more than a hot beverage warranted. "But where's yours?"

"Didn't survive the car ride," she chuckled, and instantly the tension hanging in the ice-cold air evaporated.

"That's my Grace. Slayer of cocoa and baked goods." His

eyes brimmed with affection, and he placed a gentle kiss on her forehead.

His Grace. The words gave her a thrill. She wanted to be his and for him to be hers. She'd found something magical at the most magical time of the year, and that was no coincidence.

"I like it. Might add it to my resume." The wind whisked over the top layer of snow, spreading sparkles around their legs. "So, tell me about this." She held her hand up to the partially made structure.

"I was making an igloo for us. It's seven feet in diameter, so we both have some space to stand. The snow is nice and wind packed right now, so I cut out the blocks." He gestured to dozens of rectangular-shaped snow bricks around the circle. "I was going to make a hole at the top so we could see the stars."

A little piece of her simply melted. "What's the next step?"

"You just got here. I don't want to make you work." His brow furrowed, and she nearly laughed.

"Or maybe you don't want to relinquish control of your design?" She brushed the snow from his shoulders, and grinned.

"Maybe a little." His eyes twinkled, cheeks rose.

"I won't move a flake of snow without your consent." She followed his gaze to the igloo. Now that she knew what it was, it was easy to picture how it would come together. And Owen had done the brunt of the work. His arm was going to be sore.

"Promise?" He grinned and held out his pinky.

"Ah, the contractually binding pinky swear," she chuckled. Linking fingers while wearing gloves was awkward, but they made it work.

"Phew, glad that's settled." He feigned wiping sweat from his brow. There was no doubt in her mind she'd be really sweating after they finished up. "We have to pack in the open spaces on the third row with snow, then add the fourth. The important thing is to angle the edges of the snow blocks toward the center."

"I'm on it. But not until you're sitting. Humor me and rest that arm, okay?" She smiled when he sank down right in a snow drift. Guess that's where his snow pants came in handy. She filled in the gaps with chunks of snow, smoothing it out as she went. Boots crushed through the snow from behind, and she smiled. He'd lasted two minutes and thirty seconds.

"That looks great." His woodsy scent made her toes curl in her boots. It was like standing in the center of a Christmas tree farm, enveloped in the aroma of balsam and pine.

She raised a brow in his direction. "I thought you were supposed to be resting."

"Rest time's over." He patted a fistful of snow into an open gap. "We can finish the last layer together."

"We have all afternoon." Although, in a couple hours, they'd lose the daylight.

He tapped his finger against her nose, as an off-center smile slid over his face, and her heart jumped. "Yeah, but every minute spent making the igloo is one minute less we get to spend in the igloo together."

Any oxygen remaining in her lungs evaporated. When

she'd regained the ability to speak, she cleared her throat. "Well, when you put it like that." She gave him a little hip bump and was rewarded with a low rumble of laughter.

They worked together to stack and angle the last layer, leaving a hole open at the top so they could see out. It was half past four when they finished. They stood in front of the igloo for a moment, with Owen's arms around her shoulders. Even through her heavy coat, the beat of his heart was palpable against her left shoulder blade, and his warm breath whispered over her ear. She was so comfortable wrapped in his arms, staring at the igloo they'd made, she didn't want to move.

"The first stars are coming out," Owen murmured. "Come inside and warm up for a second while I grab the wine and some glasses." Her hair feathered away from her neck as he breathed her in.

"It's so nice having you close like this." She let him have more of her weight as she sighed and dissolved into him.

"Grace." His voice was part warning, part plea, and goosebumps broke out over her back.

"Wine. Right." She cleared her throat and followed Owen to the deck and up to the slider. She stomped off her boots and stepped inside, shivering when the warmth hit her skin.

"I actually made something we can bring out too." Her voice wasn't quite steady, her mind solely focused on sitting snugly against Owen in the igloo. The thought did something funny to her brain, and the pace of her heart.

Owen disappeared down the hall, while she went to the kitchen where she'd left the cookies she'd made. Owen padded into the room with a bottle of cabernet and a thick fleece blanket tucked beneath his arm.

"You made those?" He was looking over her shoulder at the Tupperware container.

"Gingerbread girls and boys. Thought it would remind you of your childhood tradition." She'd considered bringing sheets of homemade gingerbread and all the fixings to decorate, but she didn't want to sway him to overdo it with his hurt arm. Clearly, he was up to much bigger construction tasks.

"If you get bored of marketing, you have a future in cookie decorating. They're amazing." He gave her shoulders a quick double squeeze and retrieved two glasses from the cabinet. If he'd smile like that over cookies, she'd make them for him every Christmas. Grace stilled. *Every Christmas.* She wanted that with Owen. Had fallen for him completely. *Oh, wow.*

She drew in a long breath, committing the moment to memory. "Ready?" Her voice wasn't completely level, but Owen said nothing as they tromped outside. He crawled through the entryway first, dragging the items he was holding along with him. She crouched down and smiled. Climbing into this big snow fort was like being a kid again. She slid the cookies through first, then inched her way in. Owen had spread out the soft blanket on the ground. It was much larger on the inside then it appeared from the outside. The air was much warmer inside the igloo, too, quiet and still.

"I'm still concerned about your arm, but this is pretty spectacular." She discarded her gloves and placed them next to his.

"You don't know the half of it." His gaze was so intense, she could've dissolved beneath it. He swallowed hard and began uncorking the bottle. Sultry red liquid splashed into the glasses as he poured. As he passed one of the drinks to her, their fingers brushed along the stem, and an electric current rippled up and over her skin. Their eyes held for one breath, then two, as the air swelled around them.

"Look up," he said, sitting against the wall. His arm came around her waist, turning her so she was seated between his legs, her back against his chest. She'd been curious why they'd made the hole slightly askew instead of centered, but now she understood. They had a direct view of the heavens, ablaze with thousands of tiny lights glimmering against the inky sky.

"Oh," she breathed. That's all she managed to get out as she stared awestruck at the glittering cloak above. How tiny they were compared to the vast atmosphere, and how lucky she was to be taking it all in with Owen. Out of the billions of people on earth, she'd found the person that made her heart expand with light and joy. A star arched over the sky in a glorious blaze and she gasped.

"A shooting star." Her voice was barely a whisper.

"A blessing, maybe a good luck sign." He nuzzled her neck, and her stomach expanded with warmth.

"Just a few weeks ago, I didn't know you existed." She angled her body slightly, so she could face him. "Now, having you as part of my life? It means something." She wanted to be honest with him, and maybe test the waters as to what he was feeling too.

"Grace." He shifted, placing down his wine and then hers. His fingers lightly skimmed her cheek, and threaded through her hair. He leveled his gaze, expression serious and yet touched. "It's starting to mean everything."

He leaned in, the fresh zing of his aftershave warming her insides, and gently, so gently pressed his lips over hers. She melted into the kiss, thinking in the back of her head that they fit together like hot chocolate and marshmallows. He cradled her face, the rise and fall of his breath quickening with the close contact. His mouth tasted tart from the wine; the lingering tang of warm spice and dark berries along with something uniquely him. He pulled back, a pang of loss echoing through her and pressed his forehead to hers.

When she thought about kissing Owen, she'd imagined sweet. It wasn't. That single skim of his lips against hers brought a storm spiraling to her doorstep, with whispers of happily-ever-after or heartbreak riding along the squall. Forever or too-good-to-be-true echoed in the thunder roaring in her ears. Her skin snapped with energy, and she put good sense aside and charged back into the blizzard. She moved her hands from his shoulders until her fingers were skimming over his hair, soft and slightly bristly. She grazed his lips again, shocked at the simple kiss's ability to knock the boots off of her feet.

"Everything," he murmured against her lips before she reluctantly leaned back. His pupils were swollen, darkening his irises, and the rapid pulse at the base of his jaw bounded into the tips of her fingers. And for the first time in her life, she felt like the heroine of own love story.

Chapter Thirteen

"Dream of sugar plum wishes and sweet kisses. (Not recommended during office hours.)"
—The Twelve Dates of Christmas *by Paige Turner*

F OR THE NEXT forty-eight hours, the feel of Grace's lips feathering over his replayed in Owen's mind. He'd never known skin so soft, eyes that gave away so much emotion. With Grace, close wasn't close enough. His body had melted beneath her touch, everything loose and warm while his heart went into overdrive. Pulse galloping in quick, frantic clips as he took in every sense, wanting to seal the moment in his mind. Her lips had tasted honeyed and bold, and when he moved his hands through her glorious hair, her ripe cherry scent surrounded him. One innocent kiss, and he knew beyond doubt that this woman was worth risking his heart.

The kiss had his mind wandering on another Monday morning as he sat at his desk, snow falling outside the panoramic windows, wondering how Grace's client presentation was going. After a salmonella outbreak, her firm was helping a restaurant with their public relations and rebranding. After they'd come inside from stargazing on Saturday, they relocated to the couch in front of his fireplace. They'd watched holiday movies until nearly midnight, and she'd playfully scolded him for using his sprained arm to make the igloo, but it hadn't bothered him in days. Most likely because Grace was constantly on his case about taking it slow and easy, and continuing to ice it even though it didn't hurt. He couldn't deny that being doted on, cared for by someone outside his family was a nice feeling.

In other relationships, he hadn't been able to lean on the person he was with. Not because they didn't offer, but because he was afraid of appearing vulnerable, not quite comfortable in his own skin. A few times, he hadn't planned anything special for them but dinner, and she still enjoyed spending time with him. She accepted him, liked the person he was, and that was a great feeling. He could be himself around her without thinking twice about whether she'd be bored by their conversations or think he was being a goof. It was unexpected to have this level of comfort with a woman he'd thought was so out of his league, but he still wasn't confident enough to toss *The Twelve Dates of Christmas* list altogether.

His office phone lit up, and he noticed his boss's extension. "Hello, sir?"

"Owen, will you bring those fluid dynamic documents to our meeting? For retrofitting the storm water systems at the new middle school?"

"Sure thing," Owen said before hanging up the phone. They had an important group meeting to recap and provide status updates on the projects currently in place. Owen shook his head, trying to wake up. He hadn't quite recovered from the late weekend nights he'd spent with Grace. Taking a big gulp of the bitter office coffee, he opened his drawer to retrieve the file, then stopped when his cell phone beeped in his pants pocket. Maybe Grace, letting him know how the meeting went.

Meeting was great. Signed twelve-month contract.

Yes! He was proud of her, happy for her, so he typed out the words *Amazing Grace!* And he meant it. Her job was important—helping small businesses get off the ground, troubleshooting with companies who were experiencing poor sales to get them back on track. Her firm was putting in extra hours before the holidays, which were rapidly approaching. There was a tangle of anxiety in his gut when she mentioned meeting her family when they came from Maine to visit on Christmas Day. It was a big step to meet her parents and sister, but one he wanted to take, especially because Nora's slime beasts were the reason Grace was at the toy store. He usually hosted dinner on New Year's Eve when his parents visited along with Sage, her husband, and children. This year the event would be special because Grace would be there too.

The meeting reminder on his computer flashed, and he gathered his materials and made his way down the hall. The roundtable was already half full of coworkers, their binders, coffee mugs, and cell phones spread out in the conference room. He sat in his usual spot, three chairs down from their boss, and pulled out his project list for the week. They moved around the table, each team member sharing accomplishments or challenges with various stages of building and design for clients. When he'd wrapped up his goals for the new tunnel and overpass materials, Mr. McClary stared at him instead of moving onto the next person, like he was waiting for something. He tried to recall if there was something he was forgetting, but his mind was blank.

"And what about the storm water systems that we discussed for the Westbrook School?" The boss tapped the top of his pen to his lined paper, mouth set in a thin line.

Owen drew in a quick breath through his nose and straightened as the realization crashed over him. Heat rushed to his cheeks and continued up his neck, through his scalp in the form of a thousand pin pricks of embarrassment. He'd forgotten the documents Mr. McClary asked him to bring fifteen minutes before the meeting, and now every pair of eyes in the room was waiting for his response. He prided himself on being reliable and sharp. Good grief, he couldn't stand when someone came to a meeting unprepared, and now it had happened to him. What a horrible feeling. How could've he forgotten?

"Ah…I'm sorry. I think I left those papers at my desk. I can go get them and—"

"No, no. We don't have time for that." Mr. McClary noted something on his paper—probably to reprimand his absentminded engineer—and nodded to the woman sitting on his right. "You're up next, Heather."

Owen couldn't find focus for the remainder of the meeting. Not with his own breathing and the loud roar of blood in his ears. He never forgot things at work. In his personal life, yes, but work? No way. Maybe it wasn't a big deal to some, but it was to him. Mortified. That was the only way to describe it. Today had been an off morning that started when he sat at his desk, but had a difficult time getting motivated to do anything. He supposed that was due to the late night watching more movies, eating pizza, and sharing laughs. His stomach quivered with anxiety. Work had always come first for him. It was the reason so many of his past relationships had failed. This time though, he was putting Grace first and he was already slipping up. Could he have a relationship without it distracting from his livelihood?

Nose to the computer screen, he worked twice as hard the rest of the day, desperately trying to repent for his oversight. Before Grace came into his life, he would've canceled his plans and stayed late, perfecting his documents to ensure he hadn't made any additional mistakes. Now though, he was itching to be out the door the moment his clock hit five thirty, so he could pick up some flowers for Grace to celebrate her successful day. He supposed it was a romantic gesture, but it came to him naturally. Maybe because Grace inspired those feelings inside him, or maybe it was an awareness of how—with a little give and take—their love languages could match. Something she'd helped him discover on one of their first dates with the runaway sleigh.

His coat was on, and he was ready to walk out the door when Mr. McClary flagged him down. "Owen, do you have time to look over some schematics and troubleshoot?"

Worst. Timing. Ever. How could he say no after forgetting the items his boss had specifically asked for at the meeting? He wanted to say no, but this was more than just a job to him. It was the career he'd worked toward his entire life. He didn't want his boss to think he'd gotten complacent, that he no longer cared to go above and beyond. He took a breath, reeling back the auto-yes that always broke away from his lips. "I could spend about half an hour more, or I'd be happy to take it with me and give it a look tonight when I get home."

"Great. I'll just get the file." Mr. McClary strode away, as if it were no big deal that Owen, who never turned down the opportunity to sink his teeth into a challenging project and find a solution at a moment's notice, had set boundaries. Grace made him want to find a balance between his personal life and his career, because she mattered. He'd offered an alternative to his boss, and the world was still turning, he hadn't been demoted. He'd analyze the data tonight and fill Mr. McClary in on his thoughts in the morning.

He glanced at his watch when his boss didn't return with the file. His office was just down the hall. What was taking so long? He was never this impatient, and he knew it was because Grace was waiting. Even if his boss came around the corner with the file this second, he was already on track to be late. Was he supposed to call her and let her know he was running behind? His muscles relaxed a fraction when he saw Mr. McClary's assistant, Brian, headed toward him, file in hand.

"McClary got caught on a phone call. Here's the file." Brian passed off the materials to him. "Have a good one."

"Yeah, you too."

HE ARRIVED AT Grace's door, arms full of red flowers. After two knocks, the scuff of boots against wood sounded beyond the door, along with the lock sliding open.

"There you are," she said. "I was really worried something happened to you."

"Are you mad? I got caught up at work. I'm sorry," he said on a rush of breath. He'd meant to text before he left, but he'd been in a hurry to get to her and distracted.

"I work too, so I get it. How about you let me know next time though—just a quick text—so I don't think you've turned into road pizza, okay?"

"I can do that," he agreed, sorry he hadn't remembered to when he got into his car. There was her smile, the one that was missing when she opened the door. Her gaze dropped to the crook of his elbow.

"Owen, those are beautiful." Grace's cheeks flushed, eyes more liquid gold than brown.

"So are you." He held them out, and she lifted the full bouquet to her nose, closed her eyes, and inhaled. Dark lashes fanned just over her cheeks, hair smoother than the flower petals spilled over her shoulders, and when she looked up at him, into him, his heart expanded. "Congratulations on your new client."

"That's really sweet." She took a step back so he could walk over the threshold. "I'm going to put these in water."

He watched as Grace unearthed a tall vase, added water, and arranged the flowers, her fluid movements mesmerizing him. "I thought we might do something different tonight."

She looked over her shoulder at him, brows slightly drawn. "It's been a long day for both of us. Want to get delivery and stay in?"

More than anything. Is that what she really wanted, or was she suggesting it for his sake? They'd stayed in the night before hanging out, and he'd enjoyed every second, but he didn't want to fall into the same rut as he had so many times in the past.

"We can stay in anytime. Let's do something fun." That's what she'd want, right? To do something adventurous? An expression passed over her face, one he couldn't quite read.

"Really? There's a great Chinese place right down the street." She stepped over to the center island in the small kitchen, gently setting the flowers in the center.

"I have a feeling you're going to like what I have planned." There it was again, that unreadable expression, but it was gone just as quickly as it appeared.

"Are my jeans and sweatshirt okay?" The indigo fabric clung to her legs like a second skin and made his pulse dash while her collegiate sweatshirt was cute and comfortable. *More than okay.*

"You're perfect." He held out his hand, sighing in contentment as her palm pressed against his. They tread down the apartment steps, and he opened the passenger-side door before rounding the car. They weren't going far. Twinkling lights glittered over every downtown building, in window shop displays, and over the towering evergreen that stood like a shining beacon on the city square. He parked on the street, took Grace's hand, and started toward the destination he had in mind. Every year, the square was transformed into an ice skating arena. The committee outdid themselves with the design, stringing silver lights over the rink, positioning a baby grand piano right on the ice for live music, and creating temporary parking spaces around the square for food trucks to draw additional interest. He knew Grace had a passion for food trucks and anything sweet.

"You brought me to ice skate?" Her face softened, eyes touching on all the fine details that made the place special. Thank goodness. She'd been silent on the ride over, which wasn't like Grace at all.

"I thought you might enjoy the snacks, with the ice as a side benefit." He tilted his head and grinned. Might as well have fun, because he'd have his battered and bruised body to contend with in the morning. He had a suspicion that strapping ice skates to his feet would be akin to lacing rollerblades onto a giraffe. If he fell, he'd have to make sure to do it on the side with his good arm, even though the other one was feeling just fine now.

"You know me on a very fundamental level." Her clear, melodic laugh was the most beautiful music. He always wanted to hear that laugh.

"Let's go get our skates, then we can eat all the things." He squeezed her hand as they crossed to the rental booth. She squeezed his back. This was what he'd been looking for but hadn't realized it until he met Grace. Now all he had to do was convince her he was what she'd been looking for too.

Chapter Fourteen

"And on the eleventh date of Christmas, the song of skates rang out over a frozen lake, part magic and part fate. (For the comfort of all mediocre skaters, no Olympians allowed, please.)"
—The Twelve Dates of Christmas *by Paige Turner*

G RACE GLIDED OVER the ice, crisp wind against her face, skates clicking against the smooth surface. Nostalgia climbed in her heart as the pianist's chords melded with a jovial voice belting out a festive holiday song. Other skaters slid by with varying degrees of skill; a blur of brightly colored earmuffs and tightly bound scarves, pink cheeks, and woolen hats. She turned on a dime, so free she was bursting with it, and skated back to Owen, who was still trying to find his rhythm in an adorable but uncoordinated shuffle. She'd been frustrated when they'd left the apartment. Being with Owen was everything she wanted and needed, but the dates were frankly becoming exhausting. It wasn't his fault that laundry was piling up in her bedroom, or that she'd gotten whiplash from falling asleep at her work desk, smacking her forehead against the keyboard, but Owen's dating triathlon was wearing her out.

Even when he wasn't following the list from her book,

he'd make reservations at nice restaurants or plan an activity. They always seemed to be busy. How long could they go on like this before sliding into a comfortable relationship where they were secure enough to do stuff like weekend chores together? He deserved to know that she'd written the book, but the longer she put it off, the more embarrassed she became. Yes, it was entertaining, but it had been based off of a fantasy—one that seemed totally ridiculous now. When he stopped using the list of dates, she'd planned to bring it up naturally, but that time never came. She straightened her shoulders. Tonight. She'd tell him tonight.

"Come on, you." She skated backward right in front of him, legs moving in and then curving out, and held out her hands. "How about I tow you while you get used to the feel of the ice."

"Okay," he said, linking his hands with hers. "But not too fast, because I know I'm going to end up on my backside, and I'd rather not fall at a high rate of speed."

"I think you're way overestimating my skating abilities. I can't go very fast. Especially skating backward." They circled the rink slowly, and with each inch of ice they covered, Owen's smile grew wider.

"How did you learn to skate like this?" he asked, stiffening up as they rounded a corner, hands tightening over hers.

His grip eased up when they straightened, tensed up again when a crowd of kids whizzed past, laughter ringing out and over the rink. "We had a pond behind our house. When it froze up, my parents would start a bonfire. Beth would come over to skate. My dad played hockey, so he taught me some moves."

"Like skating backward and turning." Owen's glasses were starting to fog up. It was a wonder that he could see the ice in front of him. Her heart warmed, brightened, that he trusted her to lead them around the rink. He'd understand why she hadn't said anything about the book. They'd laugh about how silly it was and move forward.

"Any triple lutzes in your repertoire?" He raised one brow and grinned through the fog.

"Figure skating jumps aren't taught in hockey." She smiled at the puzzled look on his face. "But I'm sure it would be interesting to watch." She chuckled slowly, spinning them in tight ring-around-the-rosy circles. "Just relax, loosen up," she said when he went rigid. He listened, forcing his muscles to slacken. More trust there. Who knew blind faith would feel so good? "I was obsessed with the Winter Olympics. Tried my darndest to learn some fancy spins and footwork until my mom banned it. I'd come in the house with big welts and bruising from smacking down on the ice so hard."

His laugh came in a quick snort. "I won't ask you for a demonstration then."

"Too soon for another trip to the ER?" She laughed when he scrunched up his face at the memory.

"That, and I plan to meet your mother in a week." He faltered slightly but regained his balance. "I don't want to explain why her daughter is in a toe-to-thigh cast."

"Fair enough." Holiday music continued to dance over the rink as they kept circling the ice, faster when there was a lively song and slower, closer at a slow song. The opening chords to "Let It Snow" danced in the air, and she slowed their spins until they were toe to toe. She lifted her arms to rest on his shoulders, sighed in contentment when his came around her waist. She couldn't help but to breathe him in as the pretty lyrics of being held tight all the way home swirled through her.

The activity of the ice rink melted away, until all that was left was Owen and the magical lyrics swirling around them. They stood in the middle of the rink, flurries whirling around them, and swayed from side to side in a sweet, high school dance-type shuffle. Snowflakes clung to Owen's hat and coat, but he didn't seem to care. His eyes, so, so green against all the white and silver snow, were fixed on hers. There was only one word to describe what she was feeling at the moment. *Mesmerized.* By Owen, the whirlwind of their relationship, and how connected she felt to him after such a short time.

She breathed him in as he leaned closer, never able to hold enough of the fresh balsam and citrus scent in her lungs. His lips pressed to the top of her head, an intimate gesture that was so sweet, tears stung behind her eyes. This was what she'd been waiting for, why no other person had gotten under her skin. She'd been waiting for Owen. As the notes of the song faded, the world slowly pulsed to life around them. She needed another second to get control over her emotions. The ones that had tears nearly spilling from her eyes. Not tears of sadness, but overwhelming emotion, like a chapter of her life had ended and a new, exciting one was beginning with Owen.

When they started to skate, it was apparent how crowded the ice had become while they swayed the time away in their own world. "Should we find our favorite food truck?" she asked, still leading him, gently tugging him along to shelter him from the people passing.

"Let's do it." They skated off the ice—well, she did. Owen stumbled, tripped, and found his balance by gripping her shoulders. Her laugh was lost in the cold night air as she helped him straighten out. They found a bench and unlaced their skates, trading them for snow boots. After returning their rented equipment, they made the rounds. Piping hot sweet potato sage bisque warmed them as they walked, then they found a picnic table and sat to share grilled cheese sandwiches and tacos with chimichurri sauce.

Owen's brows wrinkled as he gave one of the tacos a quizzical look. "I've never tried a taco."

"Hmm...now seems like a great time for that. Trust me?" A trickle of fear filtered through her chest. Would he still trust her after she told him that she was the author of the book? That she'd suspected he was using the list of dates that she'd created? She would never be dishonest with him, the book really wasn't a big deal, but would he see it that way?

"I do. Enough to try that taco, which is saying something." He reached up, tucked her hair behind her ear.

"Prepare to hear angels sing." She held one of the tortilla shells up to him, and he took a bite. She watched as his expression changed from wary to interested, and finally enjoyment.

A wide grin crossed his face. "I really like it." He reached for the rest of the taco.

"Thought you might." There was a lightness in her heart, the camaraderie between them even deeper than it had been before. The crowd started to thin as they ate; only a few couples and families lingered over snacks.

She sighed and rolled her shoulders. Why hadn't she told him she'd written the book earlier? The delicious food she'd eaten cemented in her stomach, and she drew in a long breath through her nose.

"I'm glad we did this. It was great." He grinned, expression open and happy.

She crumpled up her napkin, tossed it in an empty container. "It was fun. It wasn't the date though; it was you and me. How nicely we fit. How much we like and respect each other."

"Yeah, of course."

"I'm thrilled just being in your company. I hope we can do more of that, relaxing, watching television together, sharing dinner." She cringed at how wistful her voice sounded. Part of her knew he was a homebody at heart, and she was too. The work week was fast-paced, sometimes stressful, and she coveted the quiet moments she spent at home in a way she never thought possible. His smile wavered, and he searched her face. Had he really enjoyed all the dating, or was he just doing it for her and what he thought she wanted? Her stomach churned, nerves sparking to life.

"You've had fun though, right?" he said, almost too quickly.

She bit her cheek and did her best to breath normally. "Yes, of course." He relaxed a fraction, then tensed when she opened her mouth to speak.

"There's a but coming," he murmured.

"No," she protested a little too quickly. "There's no buts. Getting to know you over the past few weeks has been amazing." She drew in a breath, considering her words, then released it. "I just…this type of dating can't last forever." She smiled at him, but her throat was tight. His face drooped, hurt swarming in his eyes. She'd put that expression on his face. Her. She rushed to explain. "Being together, dating like this, it's amazing, but then there's coming back down to earth in the real world, you know?"

She extended her legs beneath the table, then pulled them back, fidgeting, not quite sure what his response would be.

"What do you mean?" Owen cleared his throat and shifted on the bench.

"When I was younger, I glorified dating. I thought romantic dates equaled a romantic future. Thought a man would come along and sweep me off my feet." She swallowed up the iced air, held it in her lungs.

"You deserve to be swept off your feet." Owen's expression shuttered, like he was bracing for the worst. What was he thinking? That she was unhappy with him? That wasn't the case at all. She was unhappy with herself for not telling him about the book earlier, and even more so, for not thinking about how much it might hurt him.

"No." She shook her head. "A relationship takes two people. Could you imagine the pressure that poor guy would face? Planning date after date, knowing if there was one slipup, it would be over?" She smiled in self-depreciation. What had she been thinking back then? She'd laughed off the silly, naive nature of the book. Until Owen had picked up a copy and decided it was a dating manual. Then it wasn't okay at all. She'd hurt someone she loved. And she did love him. "It's just that I want to give us a chance to be a real couple."

"Isn't that what we are?" His voice was hushed, barely a whisper. As quiet as the still air, and the surroundings.

"I just mean spending time together outside of dating." She made quotations in the air as she said the last word. "Hanging out at my apartment or your house. Doing everyday things like grocery shopping together, watching the news. Laundry. Couple things." She shut her eyes for a moment, attempting to soothe the anxiety welling. "I wrote a book, and it was published. After our first few dates, I noticed there were some similarities between the outings you planned and what I'd written."

"What?" Owen froze, still as a cement block. He didn't blink, didn't swallow, or even shift his hands, like he was momentarily rendered immobile.

A headache pulsed behind her eyes. She wanted a hot cloth on her forehead and a dark room. "I usually just write articles, blogs, and ad copy, but five years ago, I got this idea in my head. And I typed it out. To my surprise, an editor from a popular publishing house saw potential in the manuscript, and after five zillion edits, they published it."

"Grace," he said, suddenly on edge. "What are you saying?"

"I wrote the book you've been reading. I'm Paige Turner." The look on his face, the distrust, was soul crushing. She'd do anything to have Owen look at her like he had on the ice, with an open heart. The bitter disappointment infecting the air around them was choking.

"You…why didn't you tell me? Were you laughing at me

the whole time?" A combination of hurt and anger sparked in his eyes. It was better than the crumpled devastation from a moment ago, but the expression looked so unnatural on his face. A pang resonated in her chest. Oh, how she'd screwed up without even realizing it.

"Please don't think that. Not for one second. I never meant... I didn't think—"

"You didn't think to tell me you'd written the romance I was planning our dates around? Didn't think I wouldn't be mortified?" His neck was rigid, chin pulled back like he was ready to stand up and walk away, but he hadn't—not yet. She hated to admit that the idea of him giving up on them had hot tears stinging the back of her lids.

"At first I wasn't sure, and then I didn't know how to tell you. Most of the dates in the book could be typical winter dates." Grace glanced down at her hands.

When she turned her focus back to Owen, he let out a long, drawn-out breath. "Remember when I told you about my ex, and you said we had different love languages?" His voice sounded wrong. Hurt. She didn't mean to cause him pain. *That doesn't make it any better.*

"I remember." She chewed at her bottom lip, eyes burning as she tried to hold back tears.

Owen cleared his throat again. "Before she walked out, she nearly decapitated me with *The Twelve Dates of Christmas*. She told me to read it because I needed all the help I could get."

"I'm so sorry. You didn't deserve that."

"When we started seeing each other, I was so crazy about you that I was afraid of making a mistake, and I remembered the book. Thought it wouldn't hurt to look through it. I didn't want to bore you, and all this time you knew exactly the next action I would take. I can't believe you didn't tell me before now." Owen rubbed his chest, and there was a sinking in her gut. This wasn't going to be something a quick apology could fix. She'd broken his trust. Whatever she had to do to build it back up she would—if he ever let her close enough to try again.

"I can't either." A tear rolled over her cheek and splashed on the picnic table. "There has to be a point where dating slides into normalcy. I love doing fun things with you, but I also just want you. It doesn't matter to me if we go out or stay in. It's a lot to always be on-the-go. You need to know you're enough for me without all the dates. That just being with you and nothing else is enough." Nothing she said was getting through, and as each moment passed it became more apparent that she was losing him. "I was afraid of what you'd think of me. Afraid you'd assume I was that girl in the book that expected so much but didn't give much in return. I know real life isn't constant entertainment. It's sharing how your day was over a meal, shoveling snowy sidewalks, and running errands with the occasional date night thrown in here and there. I want to share our everyday moments. That's the life I envision. The one I want with you."

"At least if you'd told me you were Paige Turner, I would've been able to form my own opinions. I might be oblivious about dating, but I get that it's just a work of fiction. Now I feel like I haven't gotten to know you at all." His voice was flat, but she could still hear the pain there. "I can't think right now." He ran his hands through his hair in a brisk, agitated motion. "I'll take you home."

"Please don't shut me out."

"I don't think you ever let me in. Not really."

She ground her teeth, heartbeat pounding, and crossed her arms over her chest. "Don't. That's not fair and you know it. Do you think I was acting when I iced your hurt arm? When I told you how much you mean to me?" She wasn't even sure what to say now. He was hurting, and she was too. Her heart was an open wound rubbed against a copper sponge. This stung. The magical snow flurries that always seemed to follow them ceased, but her insides were quivering, a headache brewing strong and thick behind her eyes. Another tear dropped to the table, then another, until she was unabashedly bawling.

"Don't cry—"

Grace held up her hand and cut off Owen's words. She didn't want to hear the regret in his voice. Couldn't. Just couldn't right now. She pulled out her phone, sent a quick SOS text to Beth. "I'm sorry I hurt you. I'll do whatever it takes to make this right. That's how important you are to me." Silence stretched on like an endless night, until her cell phone pinged.

Almost there. Let me know who I need to lay into.

She slid one leg over the bench, stood, and slipped her other leg loose. "I'm sorry this didn't work out the way either of us were hoping."

"Where are you going? I drove you." He stood, holding his arms close to his body, every feature on his face down-turned and broken.

"And Beth is picking me up." She tossed the trash in the recycling bin.

"She doesn't need to. We should talk about this." He ran his hands through his hair again, hat forgotten at the table.

The last thing she wanted to do was say something she'd later regret, because she cared about him. "I don't want to talk right now. I…I can't." She started to stalk away, emotions too close to the surface to stay and try to smooth things over. Yes, she should have said something about the book, but his accusation that he didn't know her at all was harsh. Her vision blurred when the heavy-footed crunch of boots sounded behind her. She tried to find the right words to make him understand that there was no malice behind her knowledge that he'd read her book, but her throat was closing in, like even if she opened her mouth to talk no sound would come out.

She heard him release an exasperated breath as he continued to follow. "You might be mad at me, but you're not walking through the dark alone. Not waiting for Beth by yourself." Owen's voice was drained of energy. She'd done that to him, and it was a terrible feeling. Nearly as awful as her heart breaking into pieces, of the bone-deep cold penetrating her body. When they reached the sidewalk, Owen waited with her but neither of them were present. Both were trying to escape the sour feelings and stark silence that hung around them like a shadow. After what seemed like an eternity, but was probably only a few minutes, Beth pulled up to the curb and glared at Owen as Grace slipped in the car.

She didn't look back at him. Couldn't acknowledge that she was leaving part of her heart on the sidewalk. That it would never be whole again.

Chapter Fifteen

*"Sometimes love was a big, glossy present. Other times,
well, it was just a lump of coal beneath the tree."*
—The Twelve Dates of Christmas *by Paige Turner*

O WEN DIDN'T JUST bury himself in work, he sealed
himself off in a tomb of blueprints, schematics, and
equations. Usually the week of Christmas was pulsing with
excitement, but he'd never known a bleaker time. He'd
wrapped his nieces pixies on autopilot—the ones Grace had
ensured he found. He wanted to both smile and cry when he
remembered the mix of fascination and horror he'd felt when
she strong-armed the rude cashier into getting the second
doll from the back room before closing time. His phone had
been silent since that night at the skating rink, with only the
occasional text from his sister or a friend. Each time though,
it felt like a cruel reminder that it wasn't Grace who was
reaching out to him. That she most likely never would again.

He'd been in utter shock after she admitted to writing
the book. Said things he didn't mean because he was hurt.
The ironic thing was that Grace wanted to take the next step
toward a full-blown relationship, but he couldn't after
learning that she'd kept the book from him. No, her written
words weren't what crushed him. It was that she knew he

was using the book to plan their dates, and she'd let him make a fool of himself. The picture in his mind of Grace and Beth laughing at him behind his back was so hurtful, he'd lashed out. Said he wasn't sure who she was. And had then come to find out, being together was enough for her, sharing their lives was enough. He'd never needed a book with Grace, because she was the right person for him. Or maybe she wasn't. The Grace he thought he knew never would've concealed something like that.

He stared down at his coffee, long cold, shrugged, and took a sip. He was still in the flannel pants and long-sleeve shirt he'd worn to bed, with a bathrobe to chase away the chill he'd felt since Grace walked out of his life. It was noon, and he couldn't seem to summon the energy to do anything but sit on a barstool in his kitchen and stare into the depths of his mug. He'd called into work sick, because he was. Totally heartsick. Besides, he'd wiped every project off his plate in an effort to escape painful thoughts of Grace. He couldn't remember the last time he showered, the last time he ran the dishwasher.

The doorbell shrilled and he groaned. Unless it was the Amazon driver, he didn't want to see anyone. He shuffled to the front door, arms and legs like lead posts, and slowly drew it open.

"Good grief, Owen. You look horrific. Are you sick? Is that why you haven't returned my calls?" Sage didn't wait for an invitation before stepping inside the house. "Sadie, Selina, why don't you go up to the playroom while I talk to your uncle?"

Santa's visit imminent, his nieces started toward the

stairs. "Feel better, Uncle," Sadie said before hopping up the stairs.

"Do you have the flu?" Sage touched the back of her hand to his forehead, looking for a fever. "Come sit and tell me." He followed her to the kitchen and sat back at his stool. "How old is this coffee?"

"Not sure." He wasn't trying to be rude, but he just wanted to be alone.

She crossed over to him and glanced in his mug, sniffed the contents. "Too old is the answer." Without another word she emptied and cleaned the coffeepot, put a new filter and fresh grounds into the machine.

"Coffee's for me because I worked a double at the hospital. You need something to soothe. Tea." She filled a kettle with water, the one Owen kept at the house for her, as he wasn't much of a tea drinker, and set it on the stove. He got caught up in his own thoughts again, trying to steer them away from Grace and what she might be doing, but failed. The hiss of the kettle jarred him to the present, and Sage set a steaming mug in front of him with a click. She rounded the island and sat on the opposite side of him with her coffee. He would've preferred it, but his sister was right. The caffeine overload wasn't helping. All morning his heart had been beating in rapid succession as he considered what to do about Grace, or if it was already too late to salvage their relationship. He gripped the mug with both hands, trying to warm them. The fragrant steam rose up and peppered his nose.

"Something happened with Grace?" his sister asked over the rim of her cup. She drank her coffee black, like he did.

She used to say she wanted to be just like him. He kind of doubted that applied right now.

"I made a total fool of myself, and she let me." He scrubbed his hands over his face.

"Explain." She blew on the contents of her cup, then took a tentative sip.

"I didn't think I was enough for her. She's adventurous and bold, and I'm…Owen."

"What? You are incredible." She leveled her gaze at him with a disapproving frown. "Go on."

"You know I was using the book," he sighed.

"Yeah. It was adorable and sweet." She shrugged and rested her elbows on the countertop.

"She wrote it."

Sage's cheeks puffed out, as though she was about to spit her coffee all over the table. A hacking cough followed, but she raised her hand when he started to stand. "Sorry. That was a surprise."

"She suspected I was reading it but didn't say anything until last night." He rubbed at the nagging ache along his sternum.

"I'm sorry. She should have been upfront about it. What was her reasoning?" Sage raised a brow, steady green eyes a shade darker than his own searching his face.

"That she was afraid I'd think she was like the heroine in the book. Someone that needed a man to make her feel special with dates and surprises. That I'd think I wasn't…enough."

"Tell me everything. Maybe I can help." She settled back into her chair to listen, sipping her coffee. He told her everything. About the dates he'd planned or adapted to their argument at the ice rink. By the time he'd finished, Sage was on her second cup of coffee and had ordered them pizza. He hadn't exactly kept the house stocked with food over the week and hadn't been expecting company.

"I'm sorry. You're my best brother, and I hate how much you're hurting. I've honestly never seen a dirty dish in your sink." She glanced over her shoulder at the towering pile of cereal bowls and empty glasses.

"I'm your only brother." He rolled his eyes and took a sip of the tea just to soothe his dry throat.

"You can't let this come between you two. I know it was wrong not to tell you about the book, that it feeds right into your insecurities as a kid who was too smart for his peers to understand. As a result, you felt like you were being left out of something, picked on, which was not cool. But look at you now, Owen. You're not that adorably awkward kid. You're a successful engineer who is leaving the world a better place. You're thoughtful, bright, fun. She's lucky to have you, and I bet she knows it too, which is why she wants to start a long-term, adult relationship. In a way, what you're both feeling is kind of the same. Sounds like she was afraid that you'd see the person she once was through that book, but people grow up and change. It's part of life." She reached over the island and patted his hand. "Do you love her?"

"Of course I do. If I wasn't crazy about her, I never would've been dragged by a rabid horse or gone eighty miles an hour down a ski slope on a pool float without seat belts. Or turned molten lava into a Christmas ornament. I tried a taco, Sage." He felt more than heard the desperation in his own voice, just as the realization struck him. He'd sled all the way to work on one of those tubes if Grace would be at home when the day was done. Tame Figgy Pudding until he was running laps like Seabiscuit. Try all the heartburn-inducing food. He just wanted to be with Grace.

"You? You tried a taco?" Both his sister's brows were raised. Her mouth slightly agape.

"I ate the whole thing. It was good. I've been missing out." He raked his hands through his hair.

Sage rested one elbow on the back of her chair and looked him over. "Your life is that taco. You realize the irony of that right?"

"I don't, but I'm sure you'll tell me." He was exhausted from emotional strain and lack of sleep.

"That I will, big brother. Life's the taco. And you're Owen, who's a genius, a computer whiz, an engineer. You're amazing at so many things, and that's where you like to stay, because you're afraid of trying new things. You don't want to be disappointed. You don't want to be subpar at anything, so you don't take a bite out of the taco, out of life. And then you finally do it, and bam! It's incredible. Not everything will be like that though. You'll try things and hate them. You'll do activities that make you uncomfortable, but if you don't try, you won't know. Grace has been good for you in that way. But she also seems to know the treasure she has in you. She wants to be with you because you're awesome, not because the dates are. And you want to be with her, because..."

"She's easy to talk to, and a breath of fresh air. When I hurt my arm, she picked up so many casseroles at the market that I bought a deep freezer for the basement just so I wouldn't have to throw them away. I can tell her anything. Sometimes she'll laugh at me, but it's more with me. She just doesn't take life too seriously. She's the best friend I've ever had."

Sage was smiling at him. "I think you guys need to talk. If she's the Grace you think she is, she'll be more than willing. In fact, I bet she's in just as much anguish as you are."

"You're right. There's something I need to do. Will you help me? It's going to take a village. Literally." His stomach finally stopped twisting and churning. Having a plan always made him feel more confident. He could picture it all in his head. He just needed to click the pieces into place.

"Of course. What do we need to do?" she asked.

"Get online and search for some phone numbers." Owen had never felt more determined than he did at this moment. He was going to show Grace that he still believed in her, and trusted her by doing something he swore he never would.

Chapter Sixteen

*"That annual sweater embroidered with mallards? The
one your uncle gives you each year? Yup. That's what
heartbreak feels like."*

—The Twelve Dates of Christmas *by Paige Turner*

G RACE AND BETH walked across the parking lot of the
Windmill Lodge, avoiding the ice and slush. The frigid
gusts of wind tossed Grace's hair and seared her nostrils and
throat, icing her airways with every intake of breath. Usually,
she was bursting with excitement when her parents and sister
made the trip from Maine to Northampton, but right now
she was drained from days of trying to be strong and inde-
pendent. Every time Owen crossed her mind though, she
broke down. If this was what love felt like, it was an absolute
wonder that the human population survived. Love was awful.

"Are you sure you're up to this?" Beth laid a hand on her
shoulder as they walked. "We can tell them you're sick and
spend the afternoon eating pints of ice cream."

"As great as that sounds, we only get to see each other a
few times a year. I can stick it out for a few hours. Maybe it
will help take my mind off things." She blinked a few times
when the tears started to prickle behind her lids. *Don't think.*

"Did you tell them about how things ended with Owen?" Beth was just trying to be helpful, to anticipate her parents' questions so she wouldn't be caught off guard, but she didn't want to talk about Owen right now, or anything to do with him. It hurt too much.

"No. Hopefully it won't come up." She really, really hoped it didn't come up.

"If it does, I'll choke on my food for a distraction." Beth brought her hands to her neck and feigned gagging.

"A TRUE FRIEND." Her lips quirked slightly, the closest she'd come to a smile since she and Owen had fought at the ice skating rink. Beth must've sensed how much she was hurting, because she hadn't pressed her for more information than she was ready to give.

"You know it." Beth looped her arm through Grace's as they made their way to the revolving glass door. They both squeezed into one of the small sections of glass, slowly walking forward until they came out in the lobby of the lodge. A fire was blazing in the floor-to-ceiling stacked stone hearth, filling the space with warmth and the scent of wood smoke. She spotted her parents sitting on one of the red-and-black-checkered couches beneath an antler chandelier that hung from the soaring chalet ceiling. Her little sister had her toys lined on one of the rustic coffee tables, tawny hair tied up with a big sparkly bow that could be seen from space.

She swooped in and picked Nora up, hugging her fiercely. As always, her little sister had glitter on her fingertips from her slime obsession. "Careful those things don't excrete any goo on that table." She lifted her chin toward the toys. "Mom and Dad will have to pay a cleanup fee." She set Nora back on her feet, and Beth gave her a high-five before asking her about her slime beasts.

"Oh, honey." Her mother, Roz, held her arms open wide, and she dove into the embrace. In the safety of the hug, she was suddenly ready to break. She swallowed down the lump threatening to choke her. Tried to ignore the sharp pain wedged in her throat.

"I'm so glad you're here." Her voice was muffled by the material of her mother's sweater, soft yet durable, just like the woman herself. Fresh cotton laundry detergent mingled with the scent of her mother's favored rosewater lotion. Thank goodness some things never changed.

Her mom stepped back, held her at arm's length, and considered her. Her midnight curls carried some new raspberry-colored highlights at the tips. The one area where Roz loved variety was the shade of her hair. "I think you need an adult beverage from the bar, and then you can tell me why you look so lost."

"What am I? Chopped liver?" Her dad, a robust man in both height and width, playfully pushed his wife out of the way and swooped in. "Now who do I need to have a little chat with?" He stood back and pressed his curled fist into his meaty palm. Hands she used to call bear paws as a child.

"No one. He didn't do anything wrong. It was all me." She was still upset with herself. She really couldn't fault Owen. If their roles were reversed, she would've been hurt and defensive too. What made her sad was that Owen entertained the idea that she'd laugh at him even for one second. His lack of faith in her was disappointing. She found him fascinating, with a sharp mind fine-tuned to making things work, and bravery that wasn't immediately recognizable, but undisputable when presented the opportunity, like tackling a runaway horse or blocking a wayward sledding tube.

"Are you talking about this Owen character we were supposed to meet?" Her dad's shoulders stiffened, and he crossed his arms over his chest. He looked like he belonged at the lodge in a thick flannel shirt. She had no doubt that he hoped to have a talk with Owen, but she'd never allow it. Owen had hurt her, but it wasn't intentional. She'd hurt him too, and somehow that was worse.

"Not anymore." Her lungs narrowed, making it difficult to catch her breath. "And it's fine, really. I'd rather not talk about it." Everyone was looking at her with worried eyes. She couldn't stand the pity there. She was getting a hoard of cats. The heck with men.

"Like I said, a drink." The weight of her mom's hands compressed against her shoulders, so steady that her wound-tight muscles started to loosen and tremble.

"You go," Beth said to them. "We want to learn Nora's new slime recipe, so we're going to hang out here. Right, Mr. McGovern?" Years of knowing her parents, vacationing with them, having sleepovers gave her best friend a familial level of comfort with her parents.

"That's right. Hit it, Nora." Her dad leaned back against the plush material of the couch, not looking happy to be left out of the Owen conversation. Nora's eyes got supernova bright as she talked about the properties of slime, the different consistencies, and shimmer add-ins. Nora would've loved Owen and vice versa. They both liked to figure out how things work, and to make things better, stronger.

Her mom nudged her to the bar, and they both ordered a glass of wine. When the bartender set the long-stemmed glasses down in front of them, she took a deep breath.

"Tell me everything." Her mother angled the barstool toward her, leaving the wine for the time being. She, on the other hand, took a big gulp, the dry wine scalding her throat, raw from crying the night before.

"I don't even know where to start." Grace had never mentioned that she suspected Owen was copying the dates from her book. Her belly knotted, and she took a shallow breath. If she had asked him about the book right away, or casually mentioned she'd written *The Twelve Dates of Christmas*, all of this hurt could've been avoided. The moments they'd spent together had been so full of joy, and now it was uncertain if he'd ever forgive her.

"The point where you walked away unhappy," her mother said, eyes pained as she squeezed her shoulder. The gesture was meant to comfort, but a tear traveled slowly down her cheek, splashing from her chin and into the merlot depths of her glass.

Grace told her mother about the dates, the book, and finally the discussion at the skating rink that turned everything upside down.

"I'm sorry you're hurting, Grace." Roz brushed a tear off of Grace's cheek. "Relationships, like everything in life, are hard work. And you've never backed down from a tough job, not even when you were little. You've always known the reward at the end of your goal is much bigger than the effort it takes to get there."

Grace just nodded, unable to speak with her throat so clogged with tears. She couldn't bring herself to care what the bartender or other patrons thought. All she could think about was Owen, what he was doing, and if he was okay. Was he hurting as much as she was, or had he shrugged her off and moved on?

"You should've told him, sweetie, but you know that. And maybe Owen should've trusted your connection a bit more, and listened when you said spending time together was the only thing that was important. Should've, would've. Things you'll tell yourself over and over. Dwelling won't change anything. But you can move forward. This might be your first disagreement, but it won't be your last. Don't wait, go see him. Talk things out."

Grace hesitated for a moment, licked her chapped lips. "I'm scared he won't forgive me. That I'll lose him forever." She paused for a moment as the laughter of a large group drowned out more quiet conversations.

"I mean, I know what love looks like because you and dad have been happily married for thirty-five years. I've seen you disagree and resolve things amicably. I've never *been* in love myself though, and it's terrifying." Oh, gosh. She'd actually said it out loud, solidifying her feelings so she could no longer pretend they didn't exist. She was in love with Owen. "I don't know how to fix this. It seemed impossible to get him to hear me out at the ice skating rink."

"It's been a few days. Things always look clearer with time, and nothing you set your mind to is impossible." She gave Grace a pointed glance, daring her to object.

"Well, maybe running a marathon." She sniffled, trying to quell her tears as a group sat down on the other side of them.

"You'd never *want* to run a marathon. I know you— when you go after something that matters to you, there's no stopping until you get it. So if Owen matters, I have no doubt you'll convince him of that." Mom finally picked up her wine and started to sip.

"You're right." The bartender came over to take away her empty glass and ask if she wanted another. She declined, even though Beth was driving. She needed to stay sharp, figure out how to fix the gigantic mess she'd made by keeping the book from Owen. Tomorrow was Christmas Eve, and he'd be delivering his nieces' presents, having dinner at his sister's house. She momentarily dropped her head into her hands.

The pat of her mother's hand gently tapped her back. "We all make mistakes, honey. I know someone else who underestimates themselves. You'll turn it around. I just know it."

She sighed and massaged her temples. "I should ask him to come over. To stay in and talk things out. I should've taken care of this long before now."

"Sometimes when we're hurting we need time to process things. I find it extremely difficult to think rationally when your father goes out in that kayak and leaves his cell phone on the kitchen table—what if he got stranded or capsized? Or when he uses liquid detergent in the dishwasher and floods the kitchen with bubbles." Mom rolled her eyes, but the smile stuck.

"How many times has he done that now? And don't tell me you're not keeping track." She laughed, lightening her spirits. She'd come up with a plan to make things right.

"Seven." They both shared another laugh, then she stood up and hugged her mom.

"Thanks, I needed that." She dragged in a breath through her nose, then released it slowly through her mouth. Everything was going to be okay.

"Let's go have lunch, then you can go resolve things with Owen."

GRACE GLANCED OUT her apartment window as dusk settled over Northampton. She'd practically had to push Beth out the door fifteen minutes ago when Jim had arrived to pick her up. No way was she nestling in with the happy couple for an hour of awkwardness. They'd try to include her when everyone in the room knew they'd rather bask in the romance alone. Besides, it was time to text Owen. It was a long shot that he'd be available to talk tonight, but she'd meet him wherever he wanted. His house, her place. It didn't matter. He needed to know how she felt about him, even if he rejected her. *Please don't let him reject me.* She didn't want him to go one more minute thinking he wasn't enough for her or anyone else, or that she was laughing at him for trying to be romantic.

Hi, Owen. I hope you're doing okay. Can we talk? There are some things I'd like to tell you.

She wasn't sure what she expected, but Owen was always quick to text back, those tech-savvy fingers moving at superspeed. Not this time though. After a few minutes, she put her phone on the coffee table, picked it up to check the screen after a few more. Was he making her sweat it out? Maybe he hadn't seen the message, or maybe he was just done, plain and simple. Her phone pinged, making her jump off her seat.

I have plans tonight.

She waited for something to follow, anything, but after ten minutes, she decided to try one more time. Her shoulders rounded and she slumped against the back of the couch as she searched for something to say. This could be her only chance to convince Owen that she loved him, words that were better shared in person then through text message. She needed to see his face. To look him in the eyes so he'd see she was sincere. If he needed more time though, she couldn't push.

I understand. Be safe.

It would kill her to wait, these unspoken words burning a hole through her heart, but what choice did she have? He had every right to be upset with her, but she hoped with all her might Owen would give her that chance.

"Come on, Owen," she whispered. You know, just in case he could telepathically hear her or something. More time passed, and dusk gave way to nightfall. She didn't bother to turn on the lights. No energy for it. Instead, she sat staring out the window, silent tears running down her face fueled by the terrible ache in her chest, as streetlights cast shadows through the room. Snow had started falling again, but she couldn't muster up the typical joy it brought her to see thick flakes twirling through the air. Her mind was on Owen, and her silent cell phone.

Maybe she had lost her chance. What a tough lesson that would be. To know you loved someone, but made a mess of it. A whimper involuntarily bubbled from her throat, then the sobs came. Shoulder quaking, choking tears. She fumbled for the blanket draped over the couch and cocooned it around her shoulders, both to dash away the chill clinging to her skin and to soothe. She wasn't sure how long she sat there on the couch alone and in the dark, but a sound beyond the window had her sitting up.

A chorus of voices shared a soft holiday melody. A fair number of carolers had strolled the streets this year, a simple and touching tradition to spread joy and song, freely given with nothing expected in exchange. And wasn't that the true meaning of the holidays? If she ever got the chance, she'd give Owen the emotions in her heart whether he was ready to return them or not. On any other night, she would've rushed downstairs to listen to the music, but she wasn't in the mood. She'd most likely end up erupting into tears with all these new feelings so close to the edge. When the carolers reached the end of the song, she was relieved to have only the silence surrounding her.

Then a clear soprano voice sang out again. Grace groaned and got to her feet. She stalked over to the window and looked out at the group below, each holding long tapered candles that glowed through the dark. She squinted, looking closer. Was that Beth? Her mother and father? Even Jim and Nora? They were joined by two other children and another woman who she didn't recognize. Most likely family friends. They had plans to go caroling tomorrow night, like they always did on Christmas Eve, but it was sweet that they'd do all this to cheer her up. She rubbed her temples, trying to ease the sudden ache that throbbed there. She really did want to be alone, but their hearts were in the right place. Thanking them would only take a minute, then she could retreat to her bedroom for the night.

Grace crossed the room to the coatrack and shrugged on her jacket, patting the pocket to make sure her apartment keys were tucked away. The old stairs creaked beneath the soles of her shoes as she stomped down to the first floor. The jovial faces of her family were visible through the window, a sharp reminder of how miserable she was during the most wonderful time of the year. Her favorite time of the year. Grace pulled open the door and moved outside, giving a little wave, though everyone continued singing "Let It Snow." Of course they had to be singing the song she and Owen had been listening to last. There was a sharp pain in her chest as the memories of their time together flurried over her.

Slowly, the group began to part. Her parents and sister stepped to the left, while Beth, Jim, and the newcomers swayed over to the right. Her heart started beating more quickly, though she wasn't sure why. What were they up to? Then someone else appeared, and her breath hitched, eyes instantly blurring. Owen stepped out of the shadows, flickering candle in hand, and stepped through the break her family had made. He took one slow step, then another, until he stood a few feet in front of the others. Their eyes connected, and he held her gaze as he sang along with her family, voice clearly defined by an off-key baritone. As they neared the last verse, everyone but Owen went silent. His singing voice was so truly terrible that she had to clamp down on the smile begging to bloom over her face. The meaning of his act wasn't lost on her. It was the one date in her book that Owen said was a hard pass, because the only place his voice would blend was a haunted house (he wasn't wrong, and she loved him all the more for it). He was showing her that he trusted her enough to go outside his comfort zone. That he had faith she wouldn't make fun of him.

When the song was finished, Owen turned and handed the candle to her mother, who gave him an encouraging smile. Then he moved across the snowy sidewalk and straight into her open arms.

"Grace," he whispered, voice heavy with emotion. Pain, regret, and hope all twined within the single syllable of her name.

She tightened her arms around his neck. Nothing had been resolved, but she needed that physical contact. Sensed he needed it too. "There are things I need to say."

"Things I need to say too." His breath skimmed over her neck where she'd forgotten to wrap her scarf before coming outside. The silence suddenly struck her, and she looked over Owen's shoulder. The rest of the group had vanished without a word.

"Where did everyone go?" she asked, dropping her hands to her sides.

"The kids were promised fudge from the sweet shop around the corner, because the adults knew we'd need time to talk." He put his hands in his pockets as a gust of wind swirled silver snow around their ankles before catching his scarf and tugging it along the dancing air.

"Was that...was that your sister? And nieces?" She was choking on her own emotions. Stunned by the enormity of his gesture. What an incredible risk he'd taken, laying his heart out despite the uncertainty of their relationship, and inviting his loved ones and hers. Doing something he absolutely despised. He was giving her everything she'd wanted—a second chance at his trust, and still her heart was thrashing, her legs weak and wobbly. She was still terrified of losing him, because he mattered so much. He was bravely showing his dedication to their relationship, and he deserved no less from her. It was time to take some risks of her own.

"Will you come up?" she asked, tilting her chin toward the one glowing window on the third floor.

"I was hoping you'd ask. It's freezing out here," he said, and her teeth chattered in agreement.

Her mind was spinning with all sorts of scenarios as they walked upstairs toward her apartment. What was he going to say? How would Owen react when she told him she loved him? Would he reciprocate or run? Her heart was thundering by the time they reached the apartment door. She took a breath and gripped the brass handle.

This was it—now or never.

Chapter Seventeen

"On the twelfth date of Christmas, forever danced inside of each tiny snowflake, and whispered along the wind, as the North Star twinkled its blessing."
—The Twelve Dates of Christmas *by Paige Turner*

GRACE'S STOMACH CHURNED as she opened the apartment door and stepped inside, floorboards creaking beneath their feet. Her fingers trembled against the smooth buttons of her coat as she unfastened them, hyperaware of Owen standing behind her. Without the melody of the carolers, the apartment was silent, with only the hushed rise and fall of their breathing filtering through the air. She struggled out of the material, placed it on an open hook, pacing into the kitchen so she could get a little distance and regroup. She flipped a switch, and their little Christmas tree blazed with winding strands of multi-colored lights. The illumination left her feeling more exposed now than when they'd been standing on the dimly lit street. She needed to see him though. Try to read his expressions as they talked. She wanted him to know she was totally sincere about what she wanted to say.

With Owen right behind her, Grace crossed the room and sat at the far end of the couch near the tree, tucking her feet beneath her. She took comfort in the soft material that swallowed her up, stomach alive, quivering with the flap of nerves. Owen sat on the opposite end of the sofa so one cushion separated them. There was a vise around her heart, squeezing, constricting as she looked across at him. The low glow of the streetlights hadn't been bright enough to see his red-rimmed eyes, or the purple shadows beneath them. It pained her to look at him like this, so distraught and nervous. He sat toward her, one knee on the couch, the other foot bouncing against the floor in an uneasy rhythm. Her own face was puffy from crying, and her hair was knotted in a pile on top of her head—not the best look for a reunion.

"Owen, I'm so sorry," she began, already feeling tongue-tied despite the number of times she rehearsed the speech in her bathroom mirror.

"No. I'm sorry," he said, the wounded look on his face simply slicing through her.

"May I go first? I'm afraid I'm going to forget something." When Owen nodded, relief was a palpable thing flowing through her. She needed to get these thoughts off her chest, and if she deviated from her carefully planned speech, she'd never remember it all.

"Thank you for coming here. I don't know how you pulled it off, but your gesture floored me, Owen." Her throat was tight, and she had to force the words past the thick current of emotion. "I've been a mess. Thinking of you, replaying that night at the skating rink in my head." She dropped her gaze to her hands which were clasped tightly in her lap, nails bitten down short.

"I'm right about a lot things." She smiled, hoping to dissolve some of the tension smothering her. "But not this." She cleared her throat, forging on. "I should have insisted that the dates didn't matter instead of just hinting at it. You're the only thing that has ever mattered." She held his gaze, and he swallowed hard. "I can't take back that I didn't tell you about the book, but I promise never to keep anything from you again—except maybe the number of shoes I purchase." She gave him a little smile. "You mean so much to me, Owen." Tears blurred her vision, burned behind her eyes as she struggled to rein them in.

"You are enough." She saw Owen tense, his jaw harden. "No, not enough, Owen. You're everything. Everything to me." She moved across the couch to erase some of the distance between them. "It was never the dates creating this spark; it was the person I was with. That chemistry will be there whether we're folding laundry or paying bills, and I want that normalcy with you. I love you, Owen. You're the first person I've said those words to, and the last, if you'll forgive me for letting you down." Finally, Owen cracked a smile, and turned his wrists, palms facing up expectantly. She gripped his hands, grounding herself with the expression in his eyes.

"I'm more than willing to compromise," she continued. "To do what it takes to always put you first, to show you each day that you should never settle for being just 'enough' for someone when you can be someone's everything. My everything." Grace waited, breath hitching. It was only right for her to say the words first, when he'd shown her with his actions how much he cared. Part of meeting halfway. Part of being vulnerable, of giving a piece of yourself to another. She hadn't understood until now that Owen had always been going out of his comfort zone for her, and to put them on an equal level, she needed to be brave and do the same.

Owen lifted her hands, kissing each one before clearing his throat. "I'm sorry my own fears and insecurities had me plagiarizing the dates in your book, but I wouldn't take back a single second. This has been the most magical holiday of my life, because you're in it. I was upset when I said I didn't know the real you. I do, Grace. You bring all the sparkle. You're caring, fun, and smart. In a few weeks, you've won the title of my best friend without breaking a sweat." He took a moment to catch his breath. "I was so focused on bringing those dates to life, because I'm so scared of losing you. Who wouldn't be? I love you, Grace. There's never going to be anyone else for me. *You.*

"We're going to disagree sometimes, you'll think you're right, I'll think I'm right, but we can always meet halfway. The important thing I want you to know is I'm not going anywhere, not if you tell me you want this relationship as much as I do. You brighten up my life, Grace. You add a burst of color and lightness to every situation. I can't go back to the way things were before I met you, because you've opened my eyes to things I've never seen before. Things I've never slowed down enough to notice. I see it all clearly now, including the future we might have, and it's beautiful and full of possibility." The intensity of the love that reflected in his soulful eyes settled into her bones like a contented sigh.

She leaned in, tilting her head ever so slightly. There was a fluttering in her stomach, and an empty space only being in Owen's arms could fill. When his lips found hers, everything around her went fuzzy, but every touch, every brush of his lips was amplified.

Grace pulled back and cupped his face. "I love you, Owen. You're it for me too."

"Well, that's it then. My life has officially peaked," he said, pulling her onto his lap, holding her tight. She never wanted to be let go again.

OWEN WRAPPED HIS arms around Grace's shoulders. He could feel the quick clip of her heart bounding against his wrist. Felt his own pulse spike as he dragged in her scent, couldn't get enough of it. Less than an hour ago, he was unsure if Grace would be able to get past their argument, or decide that he was too much trouble and move on. Now she was tucked in his arms, soft and warm, soothing his fears, offering her love. Grace had been brave enough to say those three magic words first, without the assurance that he would say them back or even if he felt the same way. He straightened his shoulders, pulling her more tightly back against him, and planted a kiss in her hair. He was so proud of her for being brave, of not giving up on them. He smiled into her hair, an involuntary expression rendered from the sheer relief and joy Grace's words brought. He'd thought he lost her. He'd never take for granted the future she represented and would give his all to make it whole and bright.

On the coffee table, Grace's phone lit up. "It can wait." She shifted and nuzzled into him, resting her head on his shoulder.

He chuckled and caressed her smooth cheek with the tips of his fingers. "Beth's not going to like being left in the dark."

"How do you know it's…" She sat up with a little gasp. "Oh my gosh, I was so caught up in the moment I didn't think of anyone else." She narrowed her eyes and gave him a soft poke. "How did you coordinate it all?"

"A couple days ago I convinced Beth to give me your parents' number. Your dad wasn't happy, but he came around." He smiled, feeling quite pleased with himself. On one of their dates, Grace had mentioned where Beth worked, so he'd looked up the number to her office building and asked the receptionist to connect them. After much convincing, she agreed to give him Grace's parents' phone number. Her father was a big, scary man (he'd Googled him), and he wasn't happy in the least to hear Owen had upset his daughter. Once he had convinced him of his intentions, the man agreed to contribute to the plan.

"Days ago! I can't believe they didn't say anything at lunch today." She leaned back slightly, eyes beginning to fill despite her grin. "My dad pretended to be clueless. My mom too. And Beth! She can't keep a secret to save her life. You must have been very convincing."

"I like to think so, but more, they just wanted to see you happy." He curled in, planting another kiss on her forehead. He couldn't get enough of her. Wanted a lifetime of kisses, of drinking morning coffee together on the couch sitting just like this. His heart slapped against his ribs in an uneven beat. He knew who and what he wanted—Grace and forever.

"I am happy. So happy," she said and pressed a kiss to his

cheek. Warmth spiraled all the way down to his toes, and he savored the glow of the moment.

"Me too. My sister and nieces can't wait to meet you." Something inside him settled as she gazed at him with an expression of adoration that made him breathless.

"You mean they've been waiting all this time?" Her fingers brushed against his jawline. She kept gently touching him like she was afraid he might disappear. He understood, because he wanted to hang on, too, the lines of her body nestled against his, her scent in his lungs, silky hair beneath the pads of her fingers.

"After they went to the sweet shop. They were planning to walk back afterward." Owen was in no hurry to let her go, but the box was burning a hole in his pocket.

She stood up and extended her hand. "Let's go tell them your plan worked." He laced his fingers with hers. She still had no idea what was coming, while his insides were quivering with nerves. Once their jackets were buttoned and scarves wrapped snugly around their necks, they started down the stairs. Sure enough, the group was laughing and chatting in front of the building. The kids were forming snowballs and flinging them through the air. He gripped the warm brass handle, and opened the door so Grace could step outside. Everyone hushed. Snowballs dropped soundlessly from the children's mittens, and Grace's mother clutched her hands together in front of her chest. He'd filled them in, with the knowledge that if Grace said no to his question, his heart would shatter in front of an audience. The air was still; the only movement was the steady flakes of snow drifting to the ground.

She glanced over her shoulder as they stepped onto the powdery sidewalk. The look she gave him tossed up all of his emotions, and suddenly he couldn't recall the words he wanted to say. He took a quick step closer, fumbled when his leg slid out from under him. Owen fought to regain his balance on the slippery walkway, but Grace reached out, gripping his elbows. For one heartbeat, then two they faltered, four feet slipping this way and that. His muscles stiffened as he started to fall backward, and the motion made them both slide and crash down into a blanket of silver. He hit hard, sheltering Grace from the sidewalk with his legs. She looked at him, lips quirked.

"I think we've been in this position before." Grace's eyes were so full of humor, he chuckled, recalling their slip outside of the coffee shop. Their first date.

"Then we've come full circle," he murmured and Grace instantly sobered.

"What do you mean?" she asked, voice low and full of hope. A long shiver raced down his back, electrifying his skin, but he was no longer nervous. Everything about them fit just right. She was the missing piece to his life. The person he wanted to share everything with. Glittering flakes clung to her hair and eyelashes, her cheeks were rosy from the cold, and she was tangled up against him. This was Grace's favorite season, and he wanted to make sure it was extra special year after year.

"Grace," he whispered, hand on the outside of his jean pockets. "There's one more thing."

"What is it?" She tilted her head, a whisper of a smile playing over her lips.

Oh, she still had no idea. His heart accelerated into a frantic gallop, nerve endings tingling as the temperature sharply rose despite the glacial air.

He drew in a long breath, and leaped. "*The Twelve Dates of Christmas* aren't enough for me, because I want them all. I want to share every experience with the woman I love. Today and tomorrow. Now and for always. Grace McGovern, will you marry me?" His voice cracked with emotion, rapt attention focused solely on her. He reached into his coat pocket and took out the velvet box. "You're so full of brightness, of living, moving color, I thought your ring should be the same."

He opened the top to show her the emerald-cut ruby framed by a diamond halo. It was perfect for her, warm and vibrant. The glow of the streetlamp hit the gems at just the right angle, setting off a vision of sparkles. She placed her hands over her mouth, her eyes wide with emotion, with love and excitement. A blush spread up her cheeks, along with a brilliant smile.

"Owen." She beamed at him. "Yes. Yes! You're my everything, and I know I will never love anyone like I love you. This year and next. In this moment and forever. I don't want anyone but you." Elation spiked, crashing over him in an avalanche. She'd said yes, and together, they were going to build a beautiful life together. One of fun and laughter, of both traditions and new adventures.

Steady now, he removed the ring from its cushion and lifted it to her hands. The smooth platinum glided easily up her finger. His ring looked so, so right encircling her finger. A cheer went up from the family and friends surrounding them, everyone rushing forward at once to embrace and congratulate.

One frantic trip to the toy shop had changed the trajectory of his entire life, bringing him the incredible woman sitting in the snow beside him. No matter how many Christmases passed by, he'd always be grateful for the magical season that brought them together. Owen and Grace would share Christmas-ever-after, remembering to always keep the love and joy of the holidays close to their hearts, just as they did each other.

The End

Want more from Charlee? Check out her Christmas romance, *Home Sweet Christmas*!

Join Tule Publishing's newsletter for more great reads and weekly deals!

Acknowledgments

What a wonderful journey it has been to work with Tule Publishing. Thank you for the ongoing learning opportunities, the brainstorming phone calls, and your endless professionalism. Jane, Meghan, Nikki, Cyndi, Lee, and most of all, my wonderful editor Sinclair—thank you!

If you enjoyed *Twelve Dates of Christmas*, you'll love the next book in the…

Northampton Hearts series

Book 1: *Twelve Dates of Christmas*

Book 2: *Fourteen Days of Valentine's*
Coming in February 2022!

Available now at your favorite online retailer!

More books by Charlee James

Home Sweet Christmas

The Cape Cod Shore series

Book 1: *In With the Tide*

Book 2: *Caught in the Current*

Book 3: *Dangerous Water*

Available now at your favorite online retailer!

About the Author

Contemporary Romance Author Charlee James was introduced to a life-long love of reading listening to her parents recite nightly stories to her and her older sister. Inspired by the incredible imaginations of authors like Bill Peet, Charlee could often be found crafting her own tales. As a teenager, she got her hands on a romance novel and was instantly hooked by the genre.

After graduating from Johnson & Wales University, her early career as a wedding planner gave her first-hand experience with couples who had gone the distance for love. Always fascinated by family dynamics, Charlee began writing heartwarming novels with happily-ever-afters.

Charlee is a New England native who lives with her husband, daughter, two rambunctious dogs, a cat, and numerous reptiles. When she's not spending time with her tight-knit family, she enjoys curling up with a book, practicing yoga, and collecting Boston Terrier knick-knacks.

Thank you for reading

Twelve Dates of Christmas

If you enjoyed this book, you can find more from all our great authors at TulePublishing.com, or from your favorite online retailer.

Printed in Great Britain
by Amazon